what I thought you said

What I thought you said

Short & Shorter Stories

Mary Cuffe Perez

Epigraph Books
Rhinebeck, New York

Paperback ISBN 9781966293187
eBook ISBN 9781966293194

Library of Congress Control Number 2025917457

Cover photo by Mary Armao McCarthy
Book and cover design by Colin Rolfe

Epigraph Books
22 East Market Street, Suite 304
Rhinebeck, New York 12572
(845) 876-4861
epigraphpublishing.com

To the writers and friends of the
Pyramid Lake Women's Writing Retreat

Contents

Away

⚮

Leah drew the tip of her forefinger across the inside of the kitchen window, tracing a path, a ski trail, through the snowed-in world outside.

"Brian! Edith! Make use of yourselves!" Ruth shouted from the stove, her back turned to them as she stirred the pot of potato and cabbage soup, her voice edged with the agitation that recently cut through every word, every command. The steam and thickening broth of the kitchen were smothering, but Edith and Brian didn't seem to notice. They were too intent on their latest contest: who could tip their chair back the farthest, then shrieking when they almost fell. But now, Brian, the quickest to any command, righted his chair, rose to fetch the bread and bowls to set the table for lunch while Edith resumed her balancing feat. Leah was the youngest and not included in their latest competition, though she secretly thought of herself, at almost 11, as being much older than the two of them. She had no interest in their games. She wanted to be outside. So did Squig, who scratched at the door that led to the mudroom. No one paid much attention to him either.

It had snowed the night before, a falling of four inches, topping off the frozen layers beneath. In early December, before the deep freeze set in, the snows came in fits and starts, not enough to catch a good glide under skis. Some mornings she would wake to a few inches, on others, storms brought a heavy mix of sleet and slush. A spell of warmer days confused everything with melting, freezing, then more snow. Now, late January, winter had set in like a hen that could not be prodded off the nest. Fresh powder over enough base to lift her two feet above the same ground they would set to seed in May.

After this last snow, she would be the first to break trail, skiing up the south pasture, then gliding down toward the break in the woods and the beginning of Old Post Road that once linked farm to farm, but was fast returning to wild, except for one narrow lane through the forest that ended at Sheep Dip Pond. It was cold enough to slicken her glide and the snow deep enough that she could ski off the trail if she wished, soaring over downed trees, hummocks, and stone walls, all the way to the pond which would be locked in ice.

The image of flight was so overpowering she had already left her seat at the kitchen window and crossed to the mudroom door. Surprised by her own boldness, she turned to see her family, Edith and Brian, their bodies cupped over some conspiracy, and her mother, palms pressed to the small of her back as she often did now, staring at the wall behind the stove. If Ruth turned around, she would catch her daughter's intent. But Leah knew she would not. Her mother did not see her anymore, perhaps because she was the youngest, and Brian and Edith, with their stupid games and demands, took what their mother had to give.

It was an easy escape. She crept out without notice, Squig squeezing in behind her. The dog understood the need for secrecy and did not bark his excitement or thump his heavy tail against the mudroom floorboards. Leah held her breath as she slipped into her quilted jacket, wool mittens and cap, fastened her boots, then gathered up skis and poles.

Outside, beyond the clutch of the kitchen, the air shocked her lungs. It was colder than she thought. Colder than she had ever known it to be. A perfect day for skiing.

She snapped on her skis, pushed out a few feet, then looked back to the house, the kitchen window still steamed up, the trace of her fingertip barely visible now.

Away! she shouted, stabbing her poles into the snow, thrusting past the chicken coup, its heating lamp fogged behind the tiny window, toward the open gate into the pasture, Squig already ahead of her, trumpeting his joy. It was such easy going, even the assent to the top of the pasture—the pope's nose her father called it—her skis whistling, the air scalding cold and already icing her nose hairs, watering her eyes, making her gasp with each lungful, but good, so good, the body chugging like a heat-churning engine. Away.

At the top of the pope's nose, she stopped to gather breath and her place in the world, as she always did from here, either standing in the high orchard grass of summer, or now, in deepest winter. Late afternoons dawdling the cows home, or mornings, setting off with her father to hunt squirrel or to fish for bass in the pond, or racing sleds down the pope's nose with Brian and Edith. From here, she could see the whole of all she'd ever known—the fields undulating to the bulkhead of forest, the Helderberg escarpment beyond. At the center, the house, coup, shed, and barn huddled like bedded deer within the sugarbush of maples, the chimney exhaling into the hard blue of a January sky, just as the smoke of her own breath was taken there.

She locked her knees, leaned forward on her skis, ready to shove off down the hill and into the forest, but something held her—the unease of something left behind, or out of place. She looked back at the house, seeing her mother again, turned away. Why hadn't she spun around to catch her as she often did when one of them tried to sneak something by her. Why hadn't she stopped her from leaving? Leah could always read her mother's irritation or sadness from the way she stood at the stove, the set of her head, the angle of shoulders. What was she looking at as she stared at the wall, grease splattered with a century of cooking? What was she thinking or remembering that took her so far away? Lately, it seemed her mother had sunken somehow, sunken and then set in a way that couldn't be remade. Why didn't she turn around? Leah tossed the question off, as stifling as the kitchen's air. She sucked in the cold that blistered her throat like the taste of whisky she snitched that time, and pushed off toward the reach of blue shadow.

Away.

Out of sight. Picking up speed. If anyone was looking for her—if Ruth had turned from the stove, if Edith had wiped the steam from the window to see her outside, or Brian had thought to ask her if she'd cleaned out the coup (because he knew she hadn't)—she was beyond their reach. They could not call her back. This gave her a ferocious joy, as if she had just discovered this secret wish for escape, tucked away. Faster, skis zizzing, a dizzying blur of blue and white, then shadow, the opening into forest.

She tucked low over the skis, poles close to her sides, as she arrowed through a tunnel of snow-bent branches, slowing as the road levelled. Stopped. Squig was far behind, panting heavily, his gait lumbering. She waited for him to catch up and recover, then thrust her poles into snow, sailed through hemlocks and pines and beeches still holding last season's bleached leaves.

A cathedral of pines vaulted above her, and passing through, felt like a confession. The slant of light composed a forest of half shadow, half trees, wisps of snow between, flurries of shaved diamonds. Pole, kick, glide. Breath pumping, heart sounding to the depth of her. *Beautiful* she whispered, *beautiful.*

Tracks crossing the path. She stopped, bent to read them. A fox, traveling at a lope.

She read tracks better than her father who taught her. Knew at a glance fox from coyote, weasel from fisher. *If you follow long enough,* he said to her, *you change places. You become the followed.* He often said puzzling things and wouldn't explain them straight.

Last winter she had gone with him to hunt the fox—the same fox?—that had raided the coup the night before. They followed the tracks over a scrim of fresh fallen snow, each print a perfect arrowhead aimed at a destination, a question to be answered. Without a word between them, they tracked the fox until near dark, following over wind-thrown hemlocks, along stone walls, the tracks intersecting with the scratch and scurry of squirrels, racoons, and turkeys that passed an instant or an hour before or after. Then the fox changed direction, circled back to the pond, the ice that year too thin for them to cross.

Disappeared.

That's not what Ruth called it. *On the road,* she said, as she had many times before when he was called to haul freight. But his truck was still parked next to the woodshed. *On the road,* she'd repeat if asked again, and that was all to be said about it. Leah knew there was more. She was at the window the day he left, watched him ascend the pasture hill. It was dusk, when he should be bringing in wood for the night, but instead walked off in the opposite direction, rifle tight under his arm, spine rigid with the intent he had when hunting. He was either after the fox again or headed across the pond to poach the deer that bedded on the far side that bordered the preserve. The pond was encircled by impassable briars and rushes, and underground springs that fed the pond kept the surface from forming solid ice, except for the coldest stretch of days. It was instinct, her father told her, a kind of inner sense, that told you when the ice was thick enough to hold your weight. Was it thick enough to cross the day he left? He wore only his flannel shirt. His red and black plaid jacket still hung on the hook in the mudroom. It kept his woodsmoke smell.

She should have followed him while his tracks were fresh, before another snow had fallen. She was following him now, she realized, by instinct.

I'm not afraid, she shouted to the patches of sky above the hemlocks. *I'm not*, she repeated to Squig who cocked his head. The cinch of cold was tightening. The path that only last year had been clear to the pond had sprouted a forest of pine saplings that squeezed it to the width of a trace. *Not much farther*, she told herself, then stopped, held her breath. Leading directly in front of her were the faint depressions from ski tracks. Ghost tracks, made before the last snowfall, but examining them closely, she was surprised she hadn't picked up on them earlier and wondered how long she had been following without seeing them. She stabbed her poles into the snow, swiveled around to study the way she had come. The tracks from her own skis were all that was visible. She swung back to puzzle over the tracks leading off in front of her toward the pond. What could she make of them? She crouched down, viewing the ski tracks from a sideways angle that defined them in shadow as her father had taught her. She pulled off a mitten, traced their edges with her fingertip. They were made by someone about her own weight, she guessed, someone headed in the same direction.

She followed the tracks until the trail dwindled to a deer trace winding through alder thickets and rushes, and lost them among cattails foaming their insides out. *Just a little farther*, she told herself, pushing on through the cattails until she reached the edge of the pond. A flicker of red-gold on the opposite shore. The fox, resting on its haunches as if waiting for her. Just as she spotted him, the fox rose, and with one quick, backward glance, faded behind the rushes. She watched where the fox had been until her eyes shifted to the eruption of ice in the middle of the pond. A puzzle she could not assemble until the pieces collided into what could not be.

The Big Bang. That's what her father called the deafening roar of silence inside your head. Wreckage from a galactic explosion just getting to us now, he said. The shattered universe flooding her brain, she stared at what protruded from the ice—a flag of ice-encrusted red hair, one green and blue mitten, a ski pole half buried in snow. An inversion of what she knew to be the order of things.

Panic, her father told her, was the quickest way to kill yourself. She drew in a long, ice-edged breath, steadied. *Go back*, she said, her voice hollowed out. She stabbed her poles through snow into ice and scanned the woods, her eyes avoiding the eruption in the pond. But which way is back? Something had shifted. The sky still shone blue through the trees but she felt the pressure of coming snow. *Think!* a scream inside her head. A cut through the woods was the quickest way to the road and the opening onto the pasture. She swung around to force herself to see once more what could not be: A girl fallen through ice, half buried in snow. A question too big to carry. She left it there, then pushed out across the woods, breaking trail.

Blue gone from the sky, her breath torn into pieces. It was snowing now, falling light as a butterfly's wing, but she could feel the gathering of its intent. Her arms and legs grew heavier with each thrust of her poles. *Faster!* She cried out. It would snow her under before she reached the pasture. Where was Squig? How long had he been gone? She called, then gave the three-part whistle he never failed to answer to. A crow answered instead, a fluting call that shouldn't belong to this season.

The trail opening onto pasture. She was suddenly weight-less, exhilarated. She hardly felt the effort of skiing to the top of the pope's nose. There she stopped, intrigued by the whispering of snow as it fell upon her. The ski marks on the journey out had vanished. There was nothing, should anyone come looking, to find her by. But that time was past, she knew, even as she stood gazing at the house, the windows shrouded in steam, smoke still rising.

Back Door Shoes

～

They will be the last of her things to be taken away. The toes still wear a grin of mud and there is an attitude about them. One is turned atop the other. They could be two horses dozing in a summer field, or parent birds discussing the future of their offspring.

She had other shoes, but these were her back door shoes, slipped on in a hurry to answer what called. She wore them out. Look at them. A parody of shoes. The leather bleached and warped, the toes curled up and the sole lolling. The backs have all but collapsed where she rammed her feet incompletely into them to chase a squirrel from the birdfeeder, or a cat from the garden. There is a little knoll on the left one in the shape of a bunion. She must have stood on her toes too much.

No one would think these two with nothing much to say for themselves wore the linoleum bald with all the back and forth from the garden. They wouldn't think that the right shoe broke the kitchen window the day she flung it off in a fit; nor would they guess how many times each kicked the back door open as she came in from the garden, overloaded with tomatoes or apples or beets, cursing the weather or varmints or blight, tumbling all at the same time her load into the sink. The shoes would be pitched into the corner or crumpled beneath her as she stepped in and out of them, caterwauling to "Me and Bobby McGee" as she inspected and trimmed, washed and sorted.

They're all done now, these shoes. They don't know anything else. They will be carried out to the trash like two dead rats by whoever finds them. But for now, they remain by the back door, just where she left them. Awful with her life. Molecules of sweat and salt still singing on air.

No One Has to Sit Next to Uncle Irving

⚘

To Madeleine, the youngest, the ride to Thanksgiving never changes. For as long as she can remember, most of her eight years, the landscape from her family's house in Albany to her grandparents' house in Rochester has not deviated from what it was the year before. She knows this because while everyone else in the car—the twins, Spence and Tara, and her parents, Edmond and Roberta—argue or loudly ignore one another, she pays attention. Very close attention. Keeping everything as it has always been is her responsibility. It begins at a certain point, the exact point on I-90 when the skyline of Albany recedes behind them, past the university buildings that look like dominos about to fall, the remaining pines of the Pine Bush, the exit onto I-88, the farmland with barns going down like shot elephants, the last remaining leaves of the oaks, holding cups of granular snow they don't seem to know what to do with. In the back of the Buick is a blue and white cooler with the green bean casserole and squash pie her mother makes every year.

Thanksgiving is not Madeleine's favorite holiday, nor does it seem, is it anybody's. She is pretty sure it is not her grand-mother's either, though it's her grandparents who habitually extend the invitation for the family to gather in their small ranch house in suburban Rochester. It is her grandmother who sees to the preparations—the turkey and stuffing, the potatoes and yams and the side dishes—while sweat sheathes her forehead and drips off her nose, and her cheeks glow red as the cranberries. She becomes so ornery and probably a little drunk by the time dinner is served, everyone is glad carving the turkey is not her job.

"What I hate about Thanksgiving," Spence muses as if this is a revelation, though it is the same thing he has hated about Thanksgiving every year Madeleine can remember, "is sitting next to Uncle Irving. If I have to sit next to Uncle Irving this year, I'm moving to the little kids' table."

"I'm the one who had to sit next to him last year!" Tara shoots back.

The twins always argue about who has to sit next to Uncle Irving. And each year they campaign to detach themselves from the Thanksgiving obligation to crowd around the dining room table that, even with the extension, cannot accommodate all these people who are purported to be family though no one is sure who is cousin, aunt or uncle. They are old enough, they argue, to have Thanksgiving at a friend's house. This will never happen. They are all interned to this tradition. "Just once a year we ask you to do a family thing," Roberta replies, serving up the same rebut year after year in the same bloodless tone. "It means so much to your grandmother."

Madeleine, who is outside of these arguments, has the uneasy feeling that if anything about this tradition changes, just one small thing, it will collapse like the turkey and pilgrim inflatables that appear each year in the front yard of a trailer park a mile or so from the exit to Rochester. She does not know why this is or how to put it into words that won't be laughed at or turned into something else, but she knows nothing must change—not the structures or landscape that compose the scenery from her family's house to her grandparents' house, not the table settings with the pumpkin and turkey napkins, the feast with its centerpiece of oyster and cornbread-stuffed turkey, and someone must always sit next to Uncle Irving.

"He smells." Spence bounces this off the back of his mother's head.

"Reeks!" Tara adds in her most exasperated tone. "Like a moldy basement."

"And on his forehead, there's this humongous fat black mole sitting on top of another fat black mole . . . "

"And long, wiry hairs coming out of his ears . . . "

"Transmitters! Hacking our brains!"

"What?" Madeleine gasps, horrified.

The twins are seized by that apoplexy of laughter that jumps like an electric charge sibling to sibling. Madeleine catches it too, though she is less sure why. Being still assigned to the little kids' table, a folding card table set up in the living room, she has never had to sit next to Uncle Irving.

"But the worst," Tara sputters, "he never stops talking . . . into his stuffing!"

"Yeah! Mumbling away at the oysters, then suddenly . . . and he does this to me every year . . . he turns and stares right at me . . . spears an oyster with one of those long, disgusting fingernails . . . "

"Oh God!"

"And holds it up . . . like he just coughed up a lung!"

The two, then three, fall back against the seat in laughter that gradually trickles away. The twins drop their eyes to their phones as if summoned. There is nothing but the barrens of their destination ahead, and the drone of the car getting them there.

"Whose uncle is he anyway?" Spence asks suddenly, out of the pall that has overtaken the backseat.

Because his parents have not been listening to them, have practiced hard over the years never to listen to them, they don't answer.

"Whose uncle is he?" Tara repeats, loud enough not to be ignored.

"What?" the irritated response.

"Uncle Irving! Isn't he *your* uncle?"

"No! I don't think so." A full stop of hesitation. "He's yours, isn't he, Ed?

"Mine? Hell no, Roberta. Don't you know who's in your own damn family?"

"He must be on the other side," Roberta flicks her hand to the back seat.

"How many sides are there?" Madeleine really wants to know.

No one answers. Madeleine doesn't expect them to. She falls back against the seat and tries to find where she left off in the passing landscape. The question, however, worms its way through each mind, perhaps for the first time. Who are these people? Why do they travel to this one place to gather around a too-small table, with not enough chairs? It's always the same people—parents and grandparents, aunts and uncles and cousins. They must be family. The question grows until it becomes too heavy to think about. Something to be shrugged off, gotten out from under.

Tara resurrects Uncle Irving. "He falls asleep while he's eating. Drops his head into his plate like he's praying."

"Then he wakes up with a snort that shoots stuffing across the table.

Madeleine's attention snaps back to the twins as they complete the caricature of Uncle Irving: bald but for patches of gray hair sprouting above and out of his ears, so shrunken his head bobs above the table like a disembodied spirit, thick black eyebrows that meet in the middle like two caterpillars headbutting, capping off the feast with a sneaky green fart that clears the table.

"This year," Spence declares, "no one is going to make me sit next to Uncle Irving."

"It won't be me! If anyone tries to make me . . . "

"No one has to sit next to Uncle Irving," Roberta exhales from the front seat. "Uncle Irving won't be coming this year."

"Not on the menu," Edmond adds with a snicker.

Stunned silence in the backseat. "He's not?" Madeleine asks.

"Where would he go?" Tara wonders. "Who else would have him sit at their table if he isn't family?"

Roberta instructs Edmond, as she always does, not to follow the car in front of them so closely. Edmond doesn't seem to hear.

"Did he die or something?" Spence asks tentatively.

"Die?" Roberta responds after reminding Edmond to slow down for the exit. "I don't think so."

"Grandma didn't say? That's crazy! He's always there. Every Thanksgiving there's Uncle Irving. Every year! He's there, in the same seat at the table like he never left. I've never seen his legs!" The back seat is surprised how Spence's voice has vaulted to falsetto.

"You can sit with your cousins, Rachael and . . . Shaun?"

"Ramona and Sam", Edmond corrects a little uncertainly. They are on his side of the family, he thinks.

"You like them."

The twins go quiet trying to pull up the faces of the cousins they like. Madeleine says nothing. She realizes she has been holding her breath through the exchange and releases it into a staggering series of sighs. Something has slipped, she knows. She hasn't been paying close enough attention. She is not sure if they have passed the inflatables, or if the inflatables are still there.

She presses her forehead against the window, bares down on the landscape, the farms, the store that blinks lotto, beer and venison jerky, the garage and field of mangled and dissected automobiles, rows of boxy little houses, lights just coming on, the wide space where nothing is but a last oak, fences that keep nothing in.

A Few Lines

⌐◦

He could draw anything, anywhere. You might see him with a sketch pad balanced on his knees sitting on the stoop of a building, on a fishing pier, a subway platform, at the roadside, or there, beyond the fringe of a party.

It was never more than a few lines, so few it would seem at first glance they held nothing, but look again. It might be an old dog curled up on the sidewalk, a man leaning against a doorway, a discarded shoe. Or that girl, the one in the green dress across the room. She knows he is drawing her, and frequently glances in his direction, positioning herself in decorative poses as she chatters on with a group of admirers. He barely looks up from his sketch pad, as if he does not see her at all.

The girl is intrigued, and wants very much to see her likeness, but he, now casting his gaze across the room as if seeking another subject, seems too distant to approach. Still, she must see. She steps away from the others.

He is unaware she stands so near until she draws in a sharp breath. What she sees is no more than a few lines, a scant netting, capturing none of her poses, nothing of her. Yet it does. She sees it in an instant, but as she leans closer, the likeness unravels again. She asks him to explain, but he has no answers to offer her.

He carried nothing heavier than his box of pencils, a sketch pad when he had one, or scraps of paper, backs of envelopes, paper bags, when he did not. He was unburdened by past and future or what could be reclaimed from the dusty boxes of memory. He had no plans, no destinations. He never thought about art.

It puzzled him when people asked for explanations. He had a gift, they said, but what did his art mean? What was he getting at? He had no interpretations, no titles, nothing to fill their volumes of need. He answered with a shrug and a laugh. But their disappointment harped, pressed on his mind. He began to think about his sketches. What could he say about them? They were merely lines thrown out to catch what was there to catch. Then, to let go.

It was the letting go, he realized, that made them ask. A gift was meant to capture and hold its subject.

He was indebted to it, they said. His gift.

No longer did he sit on docks or stoops or in ditches. He rented a studio to accommodate his gift, and gathered canvases, brushes and oil paints. Thinking hard about what subject would be worthy, he found none. He passed weeks in his studio staring stupidly at the expanse of canvases, his arsenal of brushes and paints. Finally, in desperation, he returned to the girl in the green dress. His sketch had held her before releasing her. His painting would bring her back, hold her.

He dedicated himself to the making of a work of art. Lifting his brush above the simple lines of his original drawing, he felt, for the first time, the full weight of his enormous, nascent talent. His hand trembled as he added the first strokes of paint. The lines of the sketch were easily subsumed, like footprints in the sand.

Application upon application: History, anguish, vanity, hopelessness. Every stroke, another layer. Even the green dress that had been only a sweep of line in the drawing assumed its own expression. Each fold carved by the brush added to the convolution of meaning. One stroke demanded another, until the eye was trapped in a dizzying maze of complexity. The moment of self, held on the brink of flight, crushed beneath the weight of a work of art.

What I Thought You Said

～

He stares out the truck's windshield into the burrow of the trailhead, sure he is where he is supposed to be. Grunts a laugh, thinking about what he thought she said this morning: Pick me up at the Shop 'n Save. He'd misheard. She was hiking with Meredith to Hoffman's Lake. But it could be funny what he thought she said; or maybe not so funny anymore. He sighs, checks his watch. 3:45. Meredith was driving to the trailhead, but only hiking with Lily to the juncture in the trail that led to the lake. Lily would continue on to the lake and make the return trip by herself. He was to meet her back at the trailhead. At 4 pm. If he heard her right.

Mugs is already looking for her, whining and shifting from paw to paw on the truck seat beside him. The cocker used to hike with Lily, but he's old now, arthritic. "Not yet," Eliot says to the dog, running his hand over the long, silky ears, then gently flipping them back, scratches where they always itch. Mugs leans into his hand, groans softly. "Not yet," Eliot repeats to himself. But he is getting a little anxious.

She didn't say Shop 'n Save—he knows that—but maybe it was the name of another trail. He tries to think of what else sounds like Hoffman's Lake, but he can only remember the name of a few of the trails she has hiked; and there are six million acres and endless hiking possibilities in the Adirondacks. He takes a steadying breath, considers a cigarette. He should have asked her to repeat it, braved the tired, exasperated look she no longer hides. Then she'd enunciate what she'd just said in a voice so overly loud it makes him mad right back at her. "I'm not deaf," he'd reply, turning away. "Not *that* deaf."

Mugs shakes his hand away, sets his paws on the dashboard, turns to Eliot, then back to the window. Eliot knows the language, but ignores what is being asked of him. With a heavy sigh of dejection, the little dog grunts, curls up on the seat. Mugs is often disappointed in him.

There is only one other car, a jeep, parked at the trailhead. Not the perfect day for hiking. The air cold and damp, the trees, except for the oaks, nearly bare, their bark blackened from the rain of the night before. She likes to hike on contrary days like this, when there is less chance of meeting others on the trail; yet she always seems to come home with a story about someone interesting she'd met on the trail who shared some tip or bit of information useful to her—what they've seen, other trails she could try.

A wind comes up, tossing down leaves like bad cards. Did she wear her blue parka? Odd, he can't remember what she wore when she left this morning. He leans closer to the window, looks intently into the trailhead as if he could pull out the answer. The hemlocks shroud the entrance, a black vortex one could enter but not return by.

Why would anyone enter? The thought makes him shiver. November makes him shiver. A month of losses. How can you see it any other way? November strips away all illusions, lays bare how easily everything can be brought down.

He takes off his cap, runs his fingers through the thicket of white hair, then slaps the cap back on his head. When they were young, she found his wild bush of then-auburn hair delightful.

When they were young, it was always mid-summer. It was July the first and only time he hiked this trail with her.

He marks the passing of years by the animals they have had—Arrow, the Greyhound, then Foxy, a shepherd mix, two nameless cats, still alive he thinks, and now Mugs. It was back in the days of Arrow that he and Lily hiked the trail to Hoffman's Lake, before they really knew one another, back when he was still trying to keep up with her. At first, he pretended a lot, lied a lot. Told her he was as keen on the outdoors as she was, loved to cross-country ski in subzero weather, hike the highest peaks of the Adirondacks, spend a night in early April in a lean-to on Mount Marcy. They'd have frozen to death that night if Arrow hadn't crawled in the sleeping bag between them.

No matter what it was, she was always ahead of him, waiting with maddening patience, while he, breathless and physically wrung out, labored to catch up. As soon as he did, she'd throw him that brilliant, beguiling smile and be off again.

For the next few years, he maintained the illusion that he was up to it. He acquired the necessary accoutrements to at least keep her in his sights—skis, hiking boots, backpacks, a kayak and bicycle, all of which found a final resting place in the shed. If he could get away with it, he'd send the kayak down a raging cataract to oblivion. A kayak, in his judgement, was a death wish engineered from a milkweed husk. It was designed to humiliate naturally clumsy and somewhat overweight men who could not manage to get in nor out without being flipped upside down or—more mercifully—drown.

He never saw the sense in any of it. Why would you sleep outdoors when you could spend the night in a lodge, with a good book, nestled close to the fireplace? What is it about scaling a mountain or risking your life on a river that leads into lethal rapids? Why did she have to go all the way to Hoffman's Lake when Meredith had the sense to turn back?

It is 4 pm. Too early to worry. She can't be expected to be punctual returning from a 12-mile hike. It's a more or less, she always says. But the dog's up again, inserting a sharp yap between his whining. "You wouldn't keep up with her either," Eliot says but the dog gives him a quick, dismissive glance and turns back to the window. "And you know it," he continues. "You're like me." Mugs' whine becomes a kind of howl, then he turns in circles but doesn't lie down. "Or not," Eliot chuckles.

He likes books. He likes to sit in the maroon recliner with the cat-scratched armrest next to the front window and read. Occasionally, he will look out into the front yard, watch the birds at the feeder, marvel at how ingeniously the squirrels baffle the baffles. And he loves concerts, mostly classical. Lily will accompany him, but begin to fidget halfway through, as if unable to contain the energy bubbling up inside her. He likes walks, Mugs on a leash, in the park near their home where they encounter a squirrel or two, perhaps a pigeon. He prefers wildlife that doesn't surprise him.

What did they have in common? How did they come to be here? Lily off in the wilds, and he washed up on this shore, waiting for her return?

He slumps over the steering wheel, shakes his head. These are not productive inquiries, he knows. They always lead to what he fears most: that she will not return, that she will leave him for someone who shares her robust energy and love of the out-of-doors. Someone with good hearing.

He is getting a little hard of hearing, or deaf, she would say. He hears everything wrong. But it's not all on him. She talks too fast, even when she repeats herself, she talks too fast.

Often, instead of asking her to iterate what she'd said a second time, he ventures a guess, which often ends up down some dark alley of absurdity. Just yesterday, for instance, he thought she said she was going to Australia. But the look on her face told him it was one of those times when his guess took a ridiculous wrong turn. "Australia?" She shrieked, her face contorted into a question mark. "Why would I . . . " then she stopped, shook her head. "I'm going to the library! How did you get Aus . . . God!" And she turned away from him to gather her patience which had already stomped off and slammed the door.

Australia? That was an odd one to pull out of the air. Or maybe not. He hardly knew what she was thinking these days, where she might go.

When they were together, he did not worry about what she might be thinking, where she might go. They were where they should be, in the two-bedroom ranch at the end of Beecher Street, where they have lived together almost from the beginning. All the early edges had long been smoothed down. They are comfortable in their routines and habits, enjoyed the sweetness of familiar things, the neighbors, the dog. But when she is off on a hike or a kayaking trip with Meredith or with that goofy birdwatching group she belongs to, things can fall apart. He might be walking Mugs or mowing the lawn when a small but incessant doubt worms its way into his thoughts. How real was their life together? Did she love him or was she merely being kind? Did they share anything at all or was she indulging him— except for the damn hearing aid hounding.

Then, she would walk through the door, flushed and anxious to share the details of the adventure she had found, and he would pack his doubts away. The walls could be re-erected, the furniture put right, the vase of flowers arranged again on the three-legged table by the front window, dinner could be started.

OK. He needs a hearing aid. That, he hears. He knows it, but he's not ready. Has more research to do. She has done the research already, she tells him, even spoken with an audiologist. Just like her, ever on top of things. Thinks she is anyway. But she didn't catch the affair. Affair? He snorts. Nothing so rich. Back in the day it would have been called a "dalliance," if it was even that. Still, if she was so damn perceptive, you'd think she might have picked up on it.

Would he? He grabs the steering wheel, pulls himself upright in the seat. Suddenly he is certain she is having an affair. He kicks open the truck door, jumps out. "I get it," he says aloud. Looks around. No one hears.

Silence fills in around him, rings like insects in his ears. There's no one in the fucking universe to hear, he thinks. He turns back to the truck, rummages under the seat until he finds the half pack of Marlboros hidden there, leaves the door lolling open, pokes a cigarette between his lips. His eyes skim the silhouette of the distant Siamese Mountain range, then he turns back to the truck to search under the seat again until he finds a lighter. He lights the cigarette he is not supposed to have, pulls smoke into the bottom of his lungs. His mind is a storm of conspiracies: She sent me here, he reasons, but she is not here, never was. She's off with that guy she talked so much about . . . the birdwatcher . . . she'll say, when I finally catch up to her, that she never said Hoffman's Lake trail in the first place, but somewhere else. That he misheard, misunderstood. Again. *I waited,* she'll say, *but you never came. Your phone just rang and rang. You must have forgotten it. Again. Luckily, I got a ride home with . . .*

"That damn birdman!" he shouts into the abyss of the trailhead.

She was using his disability to her advantage! He throws down the cigarette half smoked. Then why does she plead with me to get a hearing aid? He paces, staring into the hash of oak, beech and maple leaves, stomps the cigarette deeper into them. He stops, balanced on a thought: Maybe it's because she knows how stubborn I am. The more she nags me about a hearing aid, the more certain she is I will resist getting a hearing aid. He swings around, faces the truck. Maybe I'll get one without telling her and then I can overhear her plans for a tryst with the birdman!

He fist pumps his logic, then sees he's left the truck door open. Mugs is gone. Panic flares. He calls but buzzing silence answers, interrupted by the slap of wet leaves blown against the truck. Frantic, he runs along the tree line calling to the dog, then back to the trailhead just as someone, then two, emerge. They stop, clearly alarmed by his agitation. A youngish couple. The woman steps back as he approaches them. He's lost his hat and he knows he must look terrifying. He holds out both hands to them as if to calm terrified animals.

"Did you see a woman on the trail? A dog? Blond. The cocker spaniel, I mean, not the woman. My wife. Her hair is brown, or mostly. His name is Mugs. The dog's I mean. She has hazel eyes and might be wearing a blue parka, but maybe not. She never dresses warm enough. She has a slight limp, but that doesn't slow her down. My wife, I mean. The dog has a limp, too. Anyway, she's beautiful. They both are." He realizes with alarm that his voice is shaking and he is almost crying. He swipes his sleeve across his face, smearing snot like a kindergartener.

"Her name is Lily."

When he says her name, his chest constricts and he staggers back a few steps. The couple look at him, alarmed. They don't know what to do. They confer, then press together as they move toward their jeep. "We didn't see her," the man mutters. "Wish we could help." But they are too unnerved to help. I must sound like a mad man, Eliot thinks as they hurry into their jeep, pull away. When he hears the tires hit the gravel of the road, he remembers he should have asked to use their phone.

It is well after 4 pm. The darkness is rising all around him. Soon it will engulf him, the truck, the trail entrance, the hills beyond. Like a drowning. He forces his panic down, tries to think straight. He has gotten it wrong. He has gotten it wrong and forgotten his phone. She could be hurt on the trail, or lost, calling to no answer.

He's lost his mind, his hearing, his wife and dog.

What did she see in him? What did they have?

When he quotes her passages from books he is reading, she will bow her head and listen with her entire self, trying to understand what it means to him; she will bake very awful pies from wild apple trees and he will always tell her how good they are; she will hold him, bring him into the fire of her body. He will wait for her, cook exquisite meals for her, or meatloaf, which is her favorite. Together, they embrace their history and their sorrows. The one they lost, the ones they had hoped for.

There is no trailhead now, the light has moved up the top of the mountain range. He will go home and get his phone, wait for a desperate call, or maybe no call, then he'll dial 911. But first he must find Mugs.

He hears the panting first, then the swish of leaves before the dog pushes through the darkness and is upon him, happy as hell. Then, Lily. She is wearing her blue parka and she is waving extravagantly, as if being rescued. She is smiling that brilliant smile and mouthing the words: I love you.

Or he thinks she is.

Shadowman

~~✦~~

R iva did not wish for the Shadowman. He appeared on his
own, wavering at the edge of the apple orchard where she
came to sit upon the stonewall and make her wish. She thought
him just another shadow until he swept out from under the sway-
ing branches of the apple trees and composed himself before her,
twirling a blossom between his fingers. He studied it quizzically.

"To be a thing," he said in a puff of wind, "a thing as sure
as that you sit upon." The petals drifted through his fingers to
alight on Riva's hands and cheeks. She realized he spoke to her.

She did not know what to say in response, though it appeared
from the tilt of his head that he expected something. Finally, he
drew in a deep breath and raised his arms. Shadows instantly
stretched beyond the trees and stirred from under the stonewall.
"How did you do that?" she asked, a little startled.

"It is what I do," he answered with a shrug. The Shadowman
was dressed in black, with a black cape that seemed to obey its
own wind. Purple-black shadows pooled under his black eyes.
He might have frightened anyone else, but Riva was used to
frightening things, and knew there was little to fear during the
day.

"Can you do it again?" she asked from her perch on the
stonewall.

The Shadowman threw up his arms and, with a pirouette,

sent the shadows leaping across the land, running through the orchard and up the hill into the cow pasture. He snapped his arms to his sides and they scurried back into place, like well trained pets.

"It's not something you do for sport," said the Shadowman. It's really quite serious business."

"I see," said Riva, puzzling this over. She slipped from the stonewall and placed her hand in its shadow. It did not move or feel like anything. Something important occurred to her. "Do you make Night?"

The shadows under the Shadowman's eyes deepened. "No. Night would come on without me. I am merely a shepherd of Night. Night is the master of all. The shadows, you see, are willful things." He scowled darkly. "I must mind them closely or they will stray, linger or bolt away." He was lost momentarily in the updraft of his cape. "Night can't be left waiting!' he roared, subduing his cape with a swipe of his arm. "When Night calls, the shadows must come as bidden."

"But in the morning . . . they come back?"

"If conditions allow, yes." A small wind teased his cape and lifted a stalk of his very black hair.

"It appears you are quite busy today." It was a brilliant day. Everything was given a shadow and the shadows grew bolder as the sun moved across the sky.

"Yes, yes, indeed," replied the Shadowman, suddenly agitated. "I can't stand here idling the day away. So, tell me, what was it you wanted?"

"Wanted?"

"Yes. Your shadow called."

Riva turned to find her shadow which, as always, was following her movements precisely. "My shadow doesn't do anything I don't do," she replied.

"It called me nonetheless."

"But wouldn't I know? It's been with me all day." Riva climbed back upon the stonewall, hugged her knees tightly to her chest.

The Shadowman swept his arms in circles as if conducting an orchestra. The shadows that had nested under the orchard spread an inch or two across the bright new grass. All the shadows in the land pulled a little away from their moorings, leaning in the direction of Night.

"Did you *whisper* a wish?" the Shadowman asked finally, admiring his work on the landscape.

"Well . . . yes," she said, a little embarrassed. Her wish was her own, and she did not want to reveal it to a stranger. "I come here to wish sometimes. This is my wishing wall."

"Well, that's it," said the Shadowman, his eyebrows lifting like two black wings. "When you wish in a whisper, you are speaking for your shadow. And I . . . being the Shadowman . . . well, I must tend my flock." Then he turned and, with a flick of his wrist, banished a shadow huddled at the base of the hill that led to the pasture. "Not yet! Not yet!" he thundered. The shadow disappeared.

"But . . . that never happened before," Riva gasped in astonishment.

"Before? Maybe *before* they weren't true wishes. Maybe you wished not to go to school or that a pony would appear in your front yard. It has to be a serious wish for your shadow to call on me."

"It is . . ." said Riva, looking down and away from the Shadowman. "But I don't know how telling you would help."

"Your shadow called me, that's all I know," said the Shadowman, growing impatient. "My flock is moving on without me." He turned this way, then that, as if something had escaped him. "Why must they be in such a hurry?!" he huffed. "As if time does not move fast enough! If I weren't here to tend them . . . well, it would always be Night, or they would not move at all, and the day would stand utterly still. I do have a little authority, you know." Then he spun around to face Riva. "As for your shadow . . . I don't know what the problem is. Only you know that." He leaned closer, his voice slithering across her face, "since you know your shadow so well."

The wind had come up again, this time with more force, and the shadows ducked into the land as if hiding from the wind's intentions. The wind gave Riva a terrible chill. She jumped from her wishing wall and approached the Shadowman who had already begun to slip away. All of herself and her shadow, too, were drawn up into the wish that came from her before she could stop from saying it.

"Tell the shadows not to hurry, Shadowman," Riva said breathlessly. She reached out for the Shadowman, then drew back, seeing he was nothing to take hold of. "Make them stay. Don't let them rush to Night." Riva was trembling and near tears. She swiped her hands across her face, embarrassed by the emotion that had overtaken her. The Shadowman paused, turned from his flock. The shadows froze in place. She knew she must explain her wish to him.

"If the Night does not come, then the dream will not come. I never want to dream again!" She did not know how to describe her dream to the Shadowman for it was beyond what words would make of it. In the dream, she found herself on the path, the same winding path she took every day. Out the blue front door of the cottage, through the creaky garden gate and up to the meadow where grew the forget-me-nots her mother loved, then across the meadow to the orchard. But when she turned to take the path back home. . . .

"A north wind," she began, finding the words, "blows it all away. I am no longer here, but lost among buildings so tall I can't see beyond them . . ." She stopped, gathered her breath. "There is no orchard, no meadow, no path to follow. . . . " She studied her hands, drew in a breath of relief. They were still plump, still young, freckled with apple tree petals. Tears filled her eyes. "I cannot find my way back." She looked up at the Shadowman, surprised by her own words. "Ah," said the Shadowman, black eyes flaring, "I see now."

"Will you help then? Will you still the Night?"

"I am only a shepherd," he replied with a touch of sadness or malice, she couldn't tell which. "Your shadow asks too much." He raised his arms and spun around so fast he became a blur, taking in sun, blossoming trees, glistening blades of grasses, and shadows, too. When he stopped, he faced Riva with a look that contained all of these. "This, my dear," he gushed, eyes glowing like coals, "*this* . . ." he bellowed . . . but the wind snatched his words away. Petals blew between them. Clouds crossed sun and rain fell in drops heavy enough to bend the blades of the new grasses.

Riva rubs the back of her hand, considers how the petals from the apple blossoms have darkened. She buries her hands deep within her coat pockets. It is cold, another season. Snowflakes fall on her cheeks. She goes dizzy watching them swirl in the street light. Only when a wind cuts cruelly through the canyon of buildings carrying the Shadowman's last words to her, does she rise from the stone steps of the library. "This," she recites, wondering which is the one door in this city she may enter, "*this* is the dream."

The Perfect Crust

~⟶

I t was a simple thing, an ordinary thing, something anyone should be able to do, but how easily it slipped out of her reach into impossibility, trailing flour and remnants of dough that never stitched into a thing to hold a pie, a thing anyone else could do.

She was always the last to arrive at the Thursday morning Coffee Cluck. Each time she rushed in on a gush of apologies the others stopped their conversation mid-stream to stare at her as if she was an intruder. She was the newest of the neighborhood group and perhaps always would be for she habitually stood at one end of the vast marble island in Mrs. Elsworthy's cathedral of a kitchen opposite the five women on the other end. On the blue-and-white-tiled walls hung brass and silver pots and implements with purposes she could only imagine.

"Oh, Violet," Mrs. Elsworthy gushed with mock enthusiasm, and, again, as if Violet was a complete surprise though she had been part of the group for close to a year now, arriving each Thursday at 10 am, or a little after in her case. They were all assembled in their customary places—Ellen Staub who appeared to lack eyelids and always stood to the right of Madelyn and Jazel, the plump, twittery twins who were not related but who Violet always saw as two of the same; and to the left of and behind the others, clutching her coffee cup as if it might save her life, the diminutive Agnes Smoles who had carefully applied lipstick to imaginary lips. Then, of course, Charlotte Elsworthy, a little apart, leaning against her stainless-steel stove that gleamed like an object of worship. Violet remembered each woman's name only by where they stood in this kitchen, and could not place them in any other circumstance.

"Coffee?" offered Mrs. Elsworthy, holding up the pot from behind a centerpiece of flagrant, orgiastic lilies. Violet shook her head emphatically. "I have decaf," Mrs. Elsworthy chirped, holding up another gleaming pot. Politely, shyly, Violet declined, offering her usual excuse about an unpredictable bladder. In truth, she was terrified of Mrs. Elsworthy. Each time she was handed one of the porcelain cups, one of Mrs. Elsworthy's grandmother's (or was it great-grandmother's?) exquisitely preserved eight-piece setting, she would be seized by an apoplexy that caused her to set the cup down on the saucer with force enough to shatter it. Mrs. Elsworthy, she could see by the tautness of her smile, knew this exactly.

Violet was certain she did not belong among these women and yet could not snap this commitment. Mrs. Elsworthy had trapped her into it a year ago by inviting Violet and her husband to brunch when they were new to the neighborhood. Really, Violet sees now, she trapped herself. She had lavishly complimented the crust of the asparagus quiche and witlessly lamented her own failed crust-making attempts. Mrs. Elsworthy's excitement at this admission—the flaring of nostrils, the snapping to of posture—should have been warning enough.

"The Coffee Cluck!" Mrs. Elsworthy clapped her hands. "Just the place for you. Oh, no, not a club. Just a cozy little cluck! In fact," she added with a pubertal pout, "we could use new members. We seem to be diminishing. One by one." She turned quickly to survey her resplendent kitchen as if one of the diminishing might be found among the Venetian dinnerware. "A few neighborhood women sharing their epicurean secrets," she sang, grasping Violet's wrists a little too tightly. "Pie crust, oh my, yes, you *must* be able to produce an acceptable pie crust."

But she never could. Each week she dutifully reported the carnage of her latest attempt to be pecked over by the five women. It was always the last topic of conversation, after the others had convulsed over their own exploits—the many uses of goat cheese, the soufflés and flans, the crème brûlées and frangipanes, and those artful hors d'oeuvres that looked like little birds settled on their nests. Violet came to resent these women for their smug, self-congratulations and for the secret they clinched tightly between their cheeks. How had they managed so effortlessly to flip the magic of flour and lard into a thing to hold volumes of fruit, with decoratively crimped edges, to boot? Golden, glistening crusts with juices sweetly gurgling out of the little V cut in the center.

Once the headiness of these accomplishments had gone a little flat, there was the customary pause, the tick of coffee cups carefully set down. Then the alight of eyes upon Violet, the perk of arousal. The twitchiness about the women's mouths told Violet it was not truly their own frothy accomplishments they had come to exalt, and not Mrs. Elsworthy's marjoram and yogurt Bliss scones. It was the doughy underbelly of Violet's failure to make a perfect crust.

Why, Violet asked herself now, gazing at the self-satisfied huddle at the other end of the marble island, did she submit to this self-flagellation, offering up just what they hungered for? Why, week after week, did she end up dragging another sacrificial failure before them, even while she hated them and herself, a hatred honed with each visit until it was as fine as Mrs. Elsworthy's French paring knives.

Not this time, Violet told herself. Today, she would simply smile into the potency of their want and offer not a word of her latest and greatest flour-flung, wall-besmirched, drain-clogging failure.

But when the moment came—after the peaks of meringue, the infusion of cardamom, the blending of roux had been conferred and put to rest and silence wrung all the air out of the room—that moment, when the women all in the same instant, turned their eyes to her—she slipped her resolve completely.

"I wanted to kill myself," she blurted at the end of yet another confessional. She had meant it—or had she?—as bemused self-mockery, but it came out crippled, a cry for help. Violet tried to rescue herself with a laugh, as if it was only a funny story, but she was beginning to feel dizzy. The arrangement of the room, the positions of the women, were disorienting. Something was out of place or missing. There was Mrs. Elsworthy a little apart from the others but always the center of things, then Ellen Staub to the right of Madelyn and Jazel. But tiny Agnes Smoles, ever hardly there, was not there. This absence was so unbalancing Violet leaned on the edge of the marble island to steady herself. The women stared at her with the hunger of hens just spying the last kernel. A low whirring rose from somewhere.

Mrs. Elsworthy stepped forward, her chin raised in a hint of triumph. "Tell us, Violet," she instructed with the excruciating patience of a ward attendant, "each step. Again. Perhaps we can find where you went wrong *this* time." Mrs. Elsworthy soundlessly settled her cup on the marble island. The others, in unison, did the same, closed their mouths, blinked.

Violet, sweating now, her voice beginning to rattle, didn't skip a detail.

Following their instructions precisely, she had measured

each ingredient to the millimeter: mincing lard into the flour until it was, as they had described, "the consistency of corn meal," shaken a handful, rather a fistful, of cold water over the dough and shaped it—yes, gently this time—without overworking as she had before, into a neat little ball, which she wrapped in wax paper and chilled for 30 minutes, no more. Yes! She had floured the wax paper generously—but not too generously like the other time—placed her dough squarely in the middle and, with lightly floured rolling pin and deft strokes, fanned it out from the center, working toward that perfect circle.

She stopped, unable to admit, once again, how it had come to the point when the center, as Yeats had written, could not hold. "What am I missing?" she gasped.

There was a moment of breath held silence. The lilies erupted. Pollen choked the air.

Mrs. Elsworthy raised an index finger, her mouth crimped tightly as if sealing in the juice of a secret. With a coy, conspiratorial wink she turned to her oven. The little group of women pivoted with her, then parted to allow Mrs. Elsworthy to genuflect before her oven and lift from it a plump, puffing pie. Holding it aloft for an instant between quilted mitts, she settled it tenderly onto a brass duvet in the center of the counter. The women leaned forward, a whirring sound rising from deep in their throats.

"There, Violet," Mrs. Elsworthy exhaled. "*That* is the secret."

The dome of crust, flushed with a hint of gold and glistening with a wash of egg white sprinkled with sanding sugar, gave Violet a strange, light-headed exhilaration. The richly tanned edges were so perfectly scalloped one would think it must be a packaged crust, if one did not know Charlotte Elsworthy. But what gripped Violet like palsy, her temples throbbing, was the rhythmic undulation of the crust, up, then down, emitting wisps of viscous steam from the dark red, oozing center. The murmur of a gurgle issued from within.

"The heart," said Mrs. Elsworthy reverently. "Without the heart, the crust has nothing to hold."

"The heart," Violet recited, smiling uncertainly. The women stared at the pie, ravenous in their unblinking gaze.

"Now," chirped Mrs. Elsworthy. She selected the appropriate knife from her cutlery board and, quivering with excitement, touched its tip to the V that puffed and gasped one last time.

Rosa

~

I t was a tragedy that Rosa did not have children of her own. This is what my mother and father, my aunt Ella and the other adults always said of her, shaking their heads. Rosa lived alone and had no family she told of. The adults spoke her name as if it was sadness itself, rocked with mirth. But I never thought sadness fit the likes of Rosa.

She came to us when I was five to care for our house and its people who were all too busy to take care of themselves. She brought King Apples grown from a tree in back of her trailer and her own cup with her name on it in gold. I remember her that first day, because she brought the outdoors inside with her.

Rosa was a river. Everything went in the direction she was going. She washed over all of the house and us. She told stories, she baked, she wore dresses with red and yellow flowers, she sang to the sheets she hung in the wind, she smelled of apples and cinnamon. She was a large woman, big enough to create her own currents.

When I was little, I swam in the river of Rosa. I believed everything she told me, was rocked by her melodies. I swung out as far as I could and back again, all on the extension of Rosa's stories and the invention of characters and places I would explore, far beyond what anyone else imagined for me.

But as I grew old enough to see beyond myself, I saw in Rosa's eyes, the children held back. I saw in her arms that cradled mending or wash or bushels of apples or other people's children, a want for her own. I heard in her laughter that washed all over me, the dry place at the end. And I saw how her laughter sprung leaks sometimes and she would set down her laundry, her mending, or rest her forehead on her wrists, her hands covered in flour, and cry like her sorrow had no end.

Rosa became too much for us as we grew older and into our own lives. We wanted less and less of her, but she was the same big river Rosa, flooding banks, yelling into everybody's business, knowing what was right. Though we ate less, she cooked more, though we no longer listened, she had more words; though we wanted her less, she held us closer, so in our escape we had to take something of her with us.

One day something in Rosa receded, pulled back by her individual moon. She gathered herself and her cup with her name on it in gold and turned away from us all. In her leaving we lived in a place a river had been, a bank holding the shape of the river, but the river gone.

Something for the Next Life

~⟍

If I believed in a permanent record, mine would have a stain on it that couldn't be left behind, no matter how far I walked away from it. A dark, red stain that seeps through every other transgression—every stolen pack of cigarettes, every lie I told to keep my balance, every promise I smashed to pieces. It spreads around me like a lake. I track it on the soles of my feet everywhere I go. It leads back to one day. The day Lavinnia told me where the baby was buried.

Maybe if I hadn't asked, I could have put it behind me, like something grown out of, and gone on to my next life, like I'd planned. Maybe it wouldn't have always been there, in the way of what might otherwise have been a regular life.

I can see us sharp as glass. The day she told me. It is 1973 and I am 14 and Lavinnia is 13. We are sitting on the front steps of 389 Swan Street, where all our plans got cooked. Where everything important to us began and ended. Lavinnia is bent over, her face bunched up in concentration as she digs furiously with her penknife into the concrete step in the space between the turned-in toes of her sneakers.

In the well, she answers in a low, hoarse voice that I can hardly hear. It is a hot day for April. Lavinnia is wearing shorts that must have belonged to one of her brothers. Everything is too small for her.

I stare at her stupidly. Like I have no idea what she's talking about.

Next to the barn, she says, not looking up.

Of course there was no barn, but I knew what she meant. She meant the barn that used to belong to her Great Grandmother's farm. There wasn't a farm, either, except in Lavinnia's Great Grandmother's mind where it existed emphatically. Lavinnia had made it a farm in her own mind, too, and she insisted I do the same. Lavinnia would give me the devil look if I made fun of Mo when she said, natural as anything, "Go fetch the rake out of the tool shed next to the barn," or "Go look back of the chicken house."

Nobody except Lavinnia and me ever visited Mo. It was easy to see why that was. Mo looked to me like one of those mummies you see in *National Geographic Magazine*. She must have been almost that old. Her back was so bent her neck ducked up out of her shoulders like a Turkey Vulture's. She was almost completely blind, but she saw the place the way it was sixty years ago with a hawk's vision. I guess it was good she couldn't see what it had become—a sunken old house with every newspaper, magazine and piece of mail she'd ever received stacked up in the corners like company that came to call and never left. Outside was just as bad. There was an over turned rabbit hutch and a chicken coop with no roof and an apple orchard that was so caught up in wild grapevine you couldn't see it anymore.

The fields that once made it a farm of nearly 90 acres had been sold off, lot by lot, and now the house sat on its own little island of once was, surrounded by trailers and modular homes that were mostly rented out.

We started going out to the farm almost as soon as Lavinnia and her four brothers moved in downstairs at 389 Swan Street. Lavinnia and I got to be best friends the first day she moved in, sitting on the front steps, having an ugly butt contest. I could spot an ugly butt coming half a block away, and I won the contest like I won most everything between us. That was the way it came to be: I was the one with the say and Lavinnia was the one who went along with whatever it was I said. Lavinnia didn't seem to mind. She was happy, I think, just to have somebody to be against the world with. She held on real tight to our friendship the whole time, right up to the end, while I hardly had to do any holding on at all.

It was my idea to visit her great grandmother's farm when she told me about it. It was just outside the city but Lavinnia didn't know how to get there on her own. It wasn't like I was going with her out of the goodness of my heart. I wanted to see what a farm was like. It was hard to believe that such a thing as a real farm with hay fields and chickens existed so close to the city. Even when I discovered it was just a farm in her great grandmother's mind, it didn't take away from the adventure of going there. I got to liking the weirdness of the place and the old mummy who lived on a farm that wasn't there. It was like being on the other side of the world to me, being in a place that didn't really exist but you could get there by bus.

After we found the well, it became a place to hide our stash, too.

Under the big maple, beside what used to be a barn, was a shallow well, banked with decaying, mossy boards, and covered with a piece of canvas because the door had rotted off long ago. There wasn't much chance anyone would happen across it, but just to be sure, we covered it with clumps of sod. We called it a well, but it was really a root cellar, Mo said, used for storing potatoes and beets and carrots. It was a perfect place to stash everything we had been collecting for the time we would light out of south Albany and the whole state of New York.

You wouldn't believe the stuff we had in there, in shoeboxes and coffee cans and wrapped in cellophane. Everything we thought we'd need when our real lives began. At the bottom was little kid stuff—make-up and nail polish and jewelry and panty hose and cartons of cigarettes. But on top was the important stuff—the radio cassette recorders that were real big at that time, and money that Lavinnia took, bit by bit from her brothers when they were too drunk to know and I, bit by bit, from Evan, my mother's new boyfriend.

It was Lavinnia's plan, the only plan I think she ever had. I just liked stealing things. But pretty soon I kind of went along with it the way I kind of went along with Mo's farm being there when it wasn't. Besides, it was a good feeling to have a plan, even if it only went so far as getting a driver's license, buying some kind of wheels and taking off. It was the taking off part that we liked best. The part we talked most about for hours sometimes on the front steps of 389 Swan Street, or in the abandoned church on Greene Street or under the maple tree at the farm. It didn't matter that we didn't know where we were taking off to. Wherever it was, whatever it led to, would be better than where we were. It would take us to our real lives. We were sure our real lives waited for us out there, maybe in South Carolina or California. We just had to get to them and then they'd start up with the roar of a Camero's engine. Eight-cylinder lives, we would have.

I'd be sitting on the front steps of the apartment building on, say, a Friday afternoon in the summer, banging my knees together with wanting to get on with something and chewing gum real hard and the next thing I knew there'd be Lavinnia beside me with that little tucked in smile that said she had something to add to the well. Then we'd be off to the farm without one word passing between us.

It took three bus transfers to get there. The bus drivers hated us. The other passengers, too, for that matter. Sometimes if the driver saw it was just us two, he wouldn't stop at all. That happened more than once, so we made sure other people were waiting at the bus stop, people the driver couldn't just leave standing there with bus fart on their face. Once we got on, the bus driver would watch us the whole time in that giant mirror that takes in the entire bus. We made a game of keeping him guessing where we were. This was a skill we were expert at.

The bus would hiss us off at Century Plaza, a grim little stretch of stores and a parking lot. The stores in the Plaza contributed a lot to the well over the years, particularly Stanley's, with its high counters that were easy to duck around. When we weren't intent on stealing some particular thing, we'd pass right through the store and out the back door, with the clerks eyeing us all the way but not interested enough to try to interfere. Then through the alley between Pettit's Garage and the Berkshire Movie Theatre, and across the yards of the little houses that squatted on the land that used to be the farm's back forty. Then we'd climb over the remains of a stone wall with fence posts sticking out of it trailing barbed wire I still have a scar from. We had worn a path through the blackberry bushes and tangle of saplings and grapevine that led right up to the back porch steps of Mo's house.

Sometimes we'd find Mo on the front porch looking out over roofs of the modular houses to the highway, rocking herself and making sounds like singing or praying under her breath.

Sometimes she'd be watching her stories on her 9-inch TV, or she might be fixing herself some fat back and cornbread on her wood stove in the parlor, which she used even though she had an electric stove in the kitchen.

I used to try to get a little rise out of her when we came in through the back door, but I never could. She wasn't like most old people. You couldn't surprise Mo. She would turn from what she was doing, real slow, and fix us with those watery, gray eyes and smile like she knew we were coming. As if we had just come from a long, long way and she had been waiting for us. I think this is why we came so often, more often than when we had something to add to the well. It was good to have somebody be glad to see us, expecting us even, and maybe wondering what took us so long getting there.

I couldn't think of anyplace else, Lavinnia says, shaking her head like it is very heavy and hard to move. She scratches a circle into the concrete step.

The summer before that afternoon in 1973, the day Lavinnia told me where the baby was buried, I stopped going to the farm with her. In fact, I didn't even come out to the front steps the entire month of August that summer even though I knew in my bones she was there, waiting for me. Things had changed over the summer. I was a whole lot better looking than Lavinnia and I knew it. I got to thinking about other things than getting out of south Albany and Lavinnia's troubles.

You see, Lavinnia's life made mine look like I took dancing lessons and owned a pony. I know she had a father who came home sometimes, but I never saw him. Her brothers were drunk all the time and meaner than sewer rats. There were times she hid in the abandoned church on Greene Street and stayed there all night, curled up on a pew, rather than go home because of what those brothers did to her. Things Lavinnia hardly even told me about, but I knew because in a way we were like one person.

Bad as things were for Lavinnia, they were going good for me that summer. My mother and I had a pretty satisfactory arrangement. She let me be most times and I let her be and that was hunky with the both of us. I'd found a serious boyfriend. Armand would come home with me whenever my mother wasn't there and we would walk right around Lavinnia if she was on the steps even though I could feel her reach right through me and grab on and hold tight in that determined way she had, but I would laugh like I didn't feel a thing and keep on going. In a way it hurt and in a way it made me feel strong and grown up, like I didn't need Lavinnia and another life, or anything we had down that well, beside a barn that wasn't there.

All the time though I could feel Lavinnia holding on tight to our friendship, like she wasn't going to let it go no matter how many times I walked past her like she wasn't there. No matter how many times she took the bus to the farm alone to add something to the well.

She held on so fierce that when I knew there was a baby going to be, we snapped back together again, tighter than before. Armand had disappeared like some magic trick, didn't even show at school, but there was Lavinnia, same as ever. It was like nothing had ever come between us and right away we got back to thinking around things as good as ever. We could think around almost any trouble we'd gotten into, though this was a whole lot bigger than getting caught drinking beer in the old church or stealing from Stanley's.

Lavinnia still hasn't looked up at me and I don't want to ask what I have to ask, because, at the time, neither of us was sure. She is digging her knife so hard into the step, her breath comes out in grunts. *Was it alive?* My voice shudders with anger or fear. "*Was it?*" I hiss into Lavinnia's wet, dirty Converse sneakers, that probably also belonged to one of her brothers at one time, with the knots that were never untied.

Her fingertips have turned white from how hard she is pressing on that penknife, until the blade finally breaks off with a tiny clink and flips down the next two steps. We stare at where it lands for what seems to be a long time until I finally look up into Lavinnia's face. That's when everything that had tried so hard to hold its place breaks apart and becomes what it would be and not what I thought I could make it be.

Strange, I don't know what she answered, or if she ever did. Everything had become something else and I got up and went upstairs and began to cry. I cried until it came out of me, because it was bound to, right there in front of my mother and her friend, Ester, who had just come over to have a few beers and trash talk and now had something bigger than she bargained for.

Maybe if I hadn't asked, I could have let it go, left it behind. Gone on to my real life that is still out there waiting for me, its engine running. But it's no use thinking about that. They took her. They took her away in her brother's shorts, both hands still clutching the penknife, dragging her dirty sneakers down the concrete steps. They took her away and she never said different. I don't know where she is now. That was in 1973. It's strange, but sometimes I get this crazy notion about going back there, to that well. Just to see what's still there. But the farm is gone, and now the old woman, too.

Before the Sale

～

Before the sale, Boone walked the land with the couple from Schenectady. They wore the wrong shoes, were unimpressed with the shaggy remaining field, complained about ticks. It was the house they were interested in, a New England farmhouse with its sweeping front porch, and the changing futures of the town, with recent upward development and a new school. They had scant interest in what had been a generational farmstead. They did not care about the history of the threshing barn, still standing straight as a good bull, or where the orchard had been with its one remaining tree, a clothesline pulley half buried in the trunk. It was his mother's, he told them, the tree and the pulley.

She hung one end of the clothesline from that corner of the house and the other end from this tree. Wash day, we'd climb to the topmost branches and pretend the sheets were the lashing sails of a ship bearing us off on open seas. My sister and brother and me.

The two grimaced up at the tree, then smiled politely.

Back then, she gave big purple-red globes, called the Apples We Tasted in Our Youth. That's one of those fancy old names folks came up with back then. Fruit so dense they popped when you sunk your teeth into them. A smack of tart and a kiss of sweet. Bushels and bushels, enough for winter stores. Now, he laughed softly, *hardly enough for a pie.*

The couple nodded indulgently, exchanged a glance. The woman turned and drifted toward the house, but Boone continued anyway, rubbing his palm over the scraggy bark like it was the hide of a favored horse soon to be put down. *This tree was here before the house, before the barn, before it was a farm at all. She's two hundred years or more.*

He could see they thought the tree looked every bit of that, a gnarled old crone, stooped and sharp clawed. Now, the man shed his pretense of patience, and followed his wife to the house. Neither looked back.

She's all knobs and hollows, he said in nearly a whisper, *but she's mother of memories and to generation upon generation of bluebirds.*

The Paper Guy

⁓

The man who brings our paper didn't deliver it Saturday. I forgave this one. The Saturday paper is an underfed thing anyway—which I have often complained to the Gazette about. But when the paper box was bereft of the fattened Sunday paper, I had to call. The paper guy—I never remember his name—gave me his home phone number when we first moved here in case I needed to halt delivery while we were away on vacation, or if I had an "issue" of any kind. That's how people refer to complaints these days. I've had plenty of issues over the years, and the paper guy, or Bob, as I later learned, heard them all. But he didn't answer the phone this time, so I left my issue with voicemail. When I didn't hear back, I called again. I was a bit flummoxed when a woman answered. I had to refer to the paper guy as just that, the paper guy, who failed to deliver the paper two days in a row.

Bob's dead. That's how she said it: *Bob's dead. A heart attack Friday after his rounds.*

I was stunned, of course. Then gushed condolences for a man I didn't know while his wife—the woman who answered the phone—said nothing. *Call the Gazette,* she said once I'd used up all my platitudes. She knew what I really wanted, the reason for my call, the only reason I had ever called. But I held my complaint about the missing papers, and I'm certainly not going to ask of a newly inducted widow, *so who's going to deliver my paper now?* Anyway, she ended the call somewhere during the long silence in which that very question swung in the air. I'm glad she happened to drop the paper guy's name before she cut me off.

Bob. Of course. Bob. Now I remember.

Bob delivered the paper. What more did I need to know about Bob? His name? Fair enough. He delivered the paper for 17 years, since the day Stan and I moved into this house. And mostly he got it right. On those mornings after one of our big Nor'easters, even before the snowplows came through, I'd see the tread marks of his rusted black jeep—Stan thought it was a pre 1990s model—leading over the snow-covered road up to our paper box, the paper left there, folded snugly inside a blue plastic jacket. Yes, mostly he got it right. Other days, for no reason I could see, the paper didn't come until after 9 am, and sometimes not at all. I let him hear it on those days, let me tell you. I had his number.

Stan didn't seem to care if the paper was late or if the paper came at all. Stan doesn't mind much. A tree could fall through the roof and he'd grunt and move into the garage. He'll read whatever's in front of him. Last week's paper all over again. That's not me. I expect to see the paper in the blue plastic jacket in the paper box with Gazette written across it in yellow letters by no later than 7:30 am. That's when I used to leave for work, an hour's drive into Albany. I'd stop at the end of the driveway, leaving the engine running, my coffee steaming away in the cup holder, look both ways just as I was told to do as a child, and cross the street to retrieve the paper. Then, the rest of the day could fall into place.

I'm retired now. The timely delivery of the newspaper is the cornerstone of my day. It's not so much what's in the paper, the news and all, but that the paper is there when I walk down the driveway each morning to fetch it. If it is late, or not there at all, it throws off my entire day. I never failed to let Bob know that.

I read Bob's obituary in the Gazette, the paper he used to deliver more or less faithfully to my paper box. Reading it, I was surprised that he had two other jobs besides delivering my paper—as a home health aide and a part-time bus driver. Seems he also volunteered at the food pantry and raised money for a summer camp for inner city kids. I knew about the summer camp. Every year, around March, he'd start with the donation letters and envelopes rubber-banded around the paper. This would go on until enough money was raised to send a bunch of kids to this camp somewhere in the Adirondacks. I never gave to that cause. I told Stan you never know where the money really goes and besides, I never got to go to summer camp so why should I give good money to let kids I don't even know raise hell at a summer camp? These fundraisers are a scam. Not that old Bob would necessarily bilk his customers but who knows? I didn't know Bob, after all.

Another thing: I never left Bob money in a Christmas card because delivering the paper was his job which he did competently enough, but I wouldn't give him a gold star, maybe a silver. I know his other customers didn't share my feelings because after the holidays he would leave a thank you letter rubber-banded to the paper, "To all of my customers who gave so generously . . ." a dig at me, no doubt.

According to the obit, Bob had another life prior to delivering the paper and before entering into these extraneous occupations that interfered with the paper being delivered on time. He'd been in the Peace Corps, apparently, engineering water retrieval systems for villagers in Africa. Where'd he learn that? He'd been a Marine, too—again, according to the obit—and later counseled vets and prison inmates. Did some kind of poetry project, if you can believe that. You have to wonder if they don't go a bit over the fence in these obits. I don't think Bob could have done all those things. But of course, I didn't know Bob.

I'd see him sometimes. If my timing was right, I'd catch him on my way down the driveway, just as he was delivering the paper. He would lean out of his jeep's window and wave the paper at me before flipping it into the box. He had a way, that flip, like it was a ballet movement or something. Or maybe just a way of letting me know, in what I suspect was a sarcastic gesture, that he was fulfilling his obligation. Then he'd blast off in a big fart of exhaust in that clattering old junker with the passenger side door secured with a bunji cord, and nudge up to the Jaworski's box. It sounds weird, but as I watched that jeep move down the road, visiting each paper box, I'd think of a fat bumblebee drawing nectar from one flower, then another. Except Bob was the giver, the box, the receiver.

The last time I saw Bob and the only time I ever spoke to him in person was two months ago. It was February. So icy I barely made it down the driveway without breaking a hip. I managed to get all the way down, but even before I got to the bottom, I could see the hungry mouth of the paper box, and no paper. No damn paper! I had a fit right there in front of the paper box, looking up and down the road to see if Bob was coming or if one of the neighbors happened to be standing at their empty paper box to share my outrage. But nothing, just the creak of groaning, ice-laden trees. I started back up toward the house, having a hell of a time, mind you, just keeping from sliding back down the driveway, when I hear the cough and rattle of that old jeep. I know it's him without turning around. I have become as attuned to the expirations of that jeep as I have to Stan's insinuations tucked inside a very bad joke. I turn and start back down the driveway. He tosses the paper across the road to me in its little blue jacket and instead of blasting off, he says the only words I'd ever heard from him face to face: "Sorry, the paper's late. Ice you know." I stand there looking at him and maybe we both smile, not sure if I did, but he did. I'm sure he did. You know what? He looked like Ernest Hemingway, at least what I think Ernest Hemingway looked like. Then he was gone, just like that, another blast of exhaust, and off he goes.

I'm going to call the Gazette. Demand that someone take Bob's route. But I haven't gotten around to it. Every morning, I walk down to the mailbox but the paper is never there. Then I look up and down the road.

The Lure

⚬

All morning, they'd fought their way through the claws of underbrush and blowdowns to get to the inlet where a small pond had formed, tucked away from the river. It was a wilder than wild place and no one came there except the pair of herons that nested in the trees on the opposite bank and the two sisters. They had followed an invisible path to find the pond. It was their secret. Or had been.

Someone was there.

A man stood on the edge of their pond where a hemlock hung low over the water. The best fishing hole.

He was a very old man, as old as their grandfather perhaps, too old to come so far into the forest. What was more astonishing was the hat he wore—a tall, black gentleman's hat from another time. It was covered with objects that threw out shocks of light though there was no sun where the man stood, deep in the shadow of the hemlock.

"Lures," whispered Agatha, the older sister. The two girls watched as the man threaded fishing line through the guides on his fishing pole. With each guide he passed line through, one or the other of the lures on his hat blinked a blue, or green, purple or silver light. The sisters were hidden by reeds as tall as themselves, but they crept closer, drawn by the lures that contained such amazements.

"How does he get them off the hat?" Farrell whispered to Agatha who knew everything.

"Like this!" sang out the man, swinging around to face where the girls hid as if they were no surprise to him. The girls drew back, stunned that he could hear them from such a distance. The man tucked his pole under his arm, raised his forefinger, elongated by a dagger-like fingernail, and lifted a purple dragonfly from his hat. It looked just like the Amethyst brooch discovered among the tangle of bright things in their grandmother's jewelry box they were told never to touch, but did. The man brought the lure down to his palm, then with a little bow, he held his palm out to the girls.

"It's alive!" shrieked Farrell, though Agatha tried to shush her.

"Is it?" The man's voice rung like a struck bell in the stillness of the forest as he considered the dragonfly in his palm. Then he pinched it between his thumb and forefinger.

The dragonfly whirred, speckling the man's face with points of purple light.

"It can catch amazing things." The man's voice slid very close. "Want to try?"

"No!" Agatha shouted. Then "no," in a smaller voice. She gripped her sister's shoulder in one hand; in the other, her fishing pole, whittled from a birch branch.

Farrell, who was in charge of carrying the bait, looked down into the coffee can and considered the squirming mass of worms. They would catch, perhaps, a little brown trout, but not amazing things, though little brown trout had been amazing to her just minutes ago as she and her sister made their way to the pond, thinking all the time of the jolt on the end of the line; then the answer: the bright thrashing body, the color of polished copper, spattered with black rain drops circled in blue. A beautiful thing, suddenly there from the brooding, opaque waters. What Farrell did not like was the way her grandfather had taught the girls how to end it. She did not like how afterwards it hung limp and unliving, no longer the answer she thought it was. A catch, nonetheless, Agatha would tell her, to be wrapped in fern and laid to rest in her creel. Then hope for another, though another seldom came.

Farrell looked up from the can of worms her thoughts had fallen into, aware now of Agatha's fierce grip on her shoulder. She twisted away from her sister so violently she fell forward, dropping her pole, worms and creel. "I don't like to be held," she yelled back at her sister. "You know I don't like to be held." But Agatha was no longer there. The man was, and suddenly too close.

"Choose one?" His voice, a cocked gun. Farrell looked back to where Agatha should be. *Agatha must be there,* she thought. *She's trying to trick me into thinking she has gone back without me. She's only hiding.*

"This one?" the man's voice broke in, holding up the zizzing dragonfly, "or any of the beauties upstairs?" His eyes flicked upward, or Farrell thought so. The hat cast a shadow that darkened the upper half of his face. Then his voice dropped like a stone. "Choose one."

Farrell went dizzy with the swirling of lights that fused, shattered, then flew back together. What were they all? Dragonflies, butterflies, beetles, even small birds? And others she could not identify, shuddery creatures she had never seen in any forest or field, their faces, in the guttering light, as human as her own.

"The purple one." She swung around, sure the voice was not her own, but from someone behind her. Agatha? When she turned back only the man was there, holding out his pole which was long and tapered, not at all like the whittled branches she and her sister fished with.

"I'll show you how to fasten it to the line."

Deftly, with one hand, he looped the line around a gleaming

silver hook. In the other, he held the dragonfly between his thumb and forefinger. "You push the hook through this part here," he said, his fingernail nicking the thorax of the dragonfly. "Then, cast it into the middle of the pond, play the line back under the hemlock. Easy as that. The insect doesn't feel a thing."

The dragonfly whirred franticly, her body coiling and uncoiling, throwing out shards of light Farrell thought would burn the skin, but the man did not seem to feel a thing.

"You will catch amazing things," he breathed, holding out to her the pole, hook and line in one hand; in the other, the dragonfly.

All she had to do was run the hook through the lure. Then, with a flick of the wrist, cast it out onto the surface of the water. The more the lure thrashes, the man instructed, the wider the circle, the surer the answer. Farrell could almost see it. A trout, the biggest ever to come from the pond. A prize, a trophy. Bring it up. Snap its neck.

She took a step forward. Her hand trembled as she reached for the lure, then her fingers drew back, reached again. Before she could touch the lure, it flashed once. Then again and again, until it flared into a blinding light, hissing a choking mist. Farrell fell backwards, gasping, submerged in the light.

When the mist cleared, Farrell sat up, breathing hard. The last of the day's light hovered in the tree tops. The man had vanished. Only the tall hat remained on the forest floor, the lures flashing and writhing as one by one they broke free of the barbs that held them.

Farrell watched as a cosmos of lights swirled around her. She wanted so much to reach out, catch one, or to have one, any one, alight on the palm of her hand, for an instant at least. But one by one they all clicked off, taking the last light with them.

Agatha must be near, waiting. Farrell didn't know the way back.

Snow in the Wrong Season

~⟋~

Beth wasn't worried. She had a long time to watch the car slow dance across the highway into the opposite lane, back again and over the embankment. She didn't feel anything.

Tomorrow, she told herself even as the car slowly spun out of her control, this won't mean anything. Just another fuck up. When the car finally came to rest, she sat patiently behind the wheel, staring through the crystalline delicacy of snowflakes on the windshield, intrigued by their determination to snow her in.

The car had landed on the passenger's side, and it struck her as funny that she had managed to remain so perfectly seated, as if this was just another approach to motoring. She didn't feel an urgency to move until snow covered the windshield, and the car's interior grew dark. Then, she unbuckled the seatbelt and, with less effort than she expected, pivoted out of the seat and shoved with her back and shoulders against the driver side door. It fell open without a sound and she stood with feet planted on the passenger side door, peering into white, surrounded by the plumbs of her breath.

She hoisted herself up out of the car. It could have been a comedy routine, where everything was done from the wrong side, like entering an exit door. Even her clothes were wrong. She wore canvas slacks and no coat and she fell several times as she struggled up the embankment in her Ducks.

It was the fastest falling snow she had ever known. When she reached the top of the bank, her pants were wet through at the knees and snowflakes hung from her bangs and eyelashes. The headlights of cars passing on the highway loomed like the eyes of giant insects, spun quickly into the web of thickening dark. She waited calmly, listening to the whisper of snow falling between the wash of passing cars. Someone would stop.

Beth hadn't expected a Mercedes, though. Unsheathed from darkness, it slipped in front of her without a sound. The passenger side door swung open immediately, emitting warmth and invitation. A glimpse of crushed leather, a soft light issuing from a dashboard of some kind of polished wood. Everything inside the car seemed slightly diffused, even the driver, who leaned across the seat and smiled up at Beth. "You need a lift it seems. Hop in."

Beth hesitated, her hand resting on the door frame while the car purred subliminally. You didn't just "hop" into such a car. "Are you sure?" she asked uncertainly. "Your car is so nice and I'm . . ." She shook her head, spraying droplets of melted snow in demonstration.

The driver laughed so quietly it was less a sound of her own than the sonorous pitch of the car's engine. "Of course," she said. "It's only a car."

Beth slid in. Even before she touched the handle, the door responded, closing her in with a little gasp. The cold rush of her presence, the snow and wetness that sprayed from her, even her own ragged breathing, dissolved into the car's muted interior.

"Sure is some car," Beth said. The driver smiled politely. Then, without glancing at the steady stream of headlights, she pulled back onto the road. "It doesn't even make a sound when you step on the gas," Beth added. "God, my Pontiac clatters like . . . " She swung around in the seat, remembering her own car's predicament. In the receding distance, one headlight journeyed obliquely into the sky. Panic clinched her throat. She should go back and turn off the headlights. Were the doors locked? Did she have the keys? These thoughts rushed at her, but couldn't quite reach her inside the swift and silent automobile.

"This a Mercedes?" Beth asked. The car looked like something from another era, yet very new.

"Oh, I don't know," the driver replied, as if the question had never occurred to her. "It's the company's car."

Beth turned again to look back at her abandoned car. She could no longer see the headlight. The battery would be dead by the time she got back.

"Just drop me at the Mobil Station," Beth leaned back into the seat that seemed perfectly molded to the shape of her body.

"I'll be glad to," the driver replied with a faint smile.

Beth studied her quickly. She might be Beth's age, or any age. There were no edges to her. The ash blond hair, beige linen suit, the opulence of the car's interior all worked together as a unit. Strange, Beth thought, that the driver had also neglected to dress for the weather. It looked as if she'd just driven in from another clime. Beth's eyes moved up to the driver's hand, posed lightly on the steering wheel, to the captive flame of the topaz ring she wore. The stone's light was unnaturally alive.

The driver caught Beth staring at her ring. "It's the company's," she said, lifting her hand from the steering wheel and extending it toward Beth.

"The company's?" Beth asked dimly. She turned away from the stone's light. The driver's hand flicked back to the steering wheel. She was squinting through the thickly falling snow.

"Here . . . I think."

"Holy shit!" Beth peered through the swipe of the blades to the darkened building. "Sorry . . . Closed," she repeated the words, printed in black scrawled letters across the glass front door. "It's like they left the country," she whispered, "in a hurry!" There was something wrong about the unlit neon sign and the reach of emptiness behind it.

"There'll be another one up ahead," the driver said, pulling into the traffic without a backward glance, the bleary lights that proceeded through the storm yielding the road to her.

"How far?" It occurred to Beth as she asked this, that she could not picture the location of the next gas station. She had not traveled east on Route 7 beyond the turn off to Route 377 for many years. Funny, she thought, how you could go one way or another way without ever thinking about it. Her whole life, it seemed to her now, happened that way.

"Only a few more miles and there's a Cumberland Farms Store. Do you have someone to call?"

"Call?" Beth slapped both palms on the dashboard. "Oh, shit! Don't tell me . . . ," she searched her pockets, the floor in front of her. "I must have left my phone ... everything ... back there." She swung around toward the driver. "Can I borrow yours?"

The driver shrugged her shoulders apologetically. "Sorry, I don't get service out here."

"Out here? How far have we come!?"

Who *would* she call? Her mother? Long dead. Warren? Long gone. Sandy? Where was Sandy? She felt caught in a gyre of faces that would not hold together, of places she could not name, of roads leading only away. This road? How many years since she'd been down this road? Twenty years maybe. Before she and Warren were married. They had come this way together once, bumping along in his old Dodge pick-up, passing a can of Schlitz, laughing or fighting. But where had it led?

"Where were you going?" Beth jumped at the driver's voice.

"When you ran off the road?" Beth looked down at her hands curled in her lap like two small sleeping animals, over to the topaz ring that flashed from the driver's finger that tapped upon the steering wheel, as if keeping time to some tune in her head. With effort, she pulled herself back to the question.

"Oh. I was on my way home." The word 'home' jerked her upright in her seat. She peered into the tunnel of snow thrown blackness. The road seemed to be only a projection of the car. "Home," she repeated, struggling with a shapeless sense of urgency. "It was just beginning to snow when I left work, but then it came faster and faster. I didn't realize how slippery it was. I tried to make the turn at the intersection. That's where I got into trouble. I slid right through it and all over the place." Beth was weaving her arms around to demonstrate the actions of the car. "The more I turned, the worse it got and then there I was in the ditch."

"And here you are!"

Beth nodded, looking around herself, surprised all over again by her surroundings. "And here I am."

They drove in silence for a moment, gazing straight ahead into the swirling vortex of snow.

"Where are you headed?" Beth asked, suddenly over-whelmed by fatigue as she stared into the tunnel, concentrating against her will on the motion of the wipers.

"Home, too."

Beth tried to envision the driver's house, but could not. She imagined it changing aspect with each suit of clothes or shade of hair she chose.

"I've been on the road all week," she sighed. "For the company."

"The company?"

"The Jewelers."

"You work for a jeweler?" Beth asked, confused. She had imagined the woman born of and sustained by independent wealth.

"*The* Jewelers," she emphasized. "We carry only the finest. You've heard of The Jewelers, surely?" She looked at Beth expectantly with a suggestion of something just beyond Beth's understanding.

"Sorry," Beth shrugged, "never heard of it." The driver's eyes hung on her a moment longer before returning to the road.

"So you sell jewelry," Beth asked after a while. "Real stuff?"

The driver looked puzzled, then tossed her head to the side and laughed gently, as if Beth had said something inadvertently clever. "I'm sorry," the driver said, her eyes still full of amusement. "I don't mean to be rude. But I thought you knew." She took a deep breath and stared into the oncoming darkness. "Yes, it's real."

Beth had the uneasy feeling she had entirely missed the point. "So ... you're like a travelling salesperson ... for jewelry?" This seemed as improbable as snow in July.

"My case is in the back there ... " the driver began. Then, "Oh! Here we are." The car slowed. Beth peered through the slanting snowfall, illuminated by the fuzzy light of a street lamp above a dimly lit building.

Beth read the words slowly, "Closed ... for ... renovations." She gripped the dashboard and turned in alarm to the driver. "I can't believe it."

The car eased past the building and back onto the highway. "Now I'm really taking you out of your way," the driver said. Do you want me to turn back? I will if you prefer. But there's a little grocery store only a few miles on. You can make a call from there. It's just before my turn off. It's up to you, of course."

"Let's go on then," Beth answered wearily.

The timbre of the engine deepened as the car accelerated. For several minutes, neither spoke. Beth felt herself sinking beneath the crushing weight of fatigue. "Is someone waiting for you?" the driver asked suddenly.

The voice, like the car, coming out of a fuddle of snow and lights. Beth gasped as if surfacing for air. She gripped the dashboard and peered at the road ahead. The snow seemed impenetrable, but through the swipes of the wipers she was sure she saw a figure ahead. "Something is out there," she said, her voice broken, not her own.

Sandy. Nine years old, waiting for Beth to come home. She had promised to be home early. In time to visit Mrs. Drawbridge's apple tree. It was older than Mrs. Drawbridge, older than the house she lived in, but it still gave big, purple-red apples. Mrs. Drawbridge could no longer gather them. Sandy and Beth would climb the tree and shake down the apples for her and carry a bushel home between them. Where the hell was she?

Beth felt something fall away inside her. She released the dashboard and settled back in the seat with a long, ragged sigh. "No, there's nothing there."

Strange, she thought, how that urgency still shadowed her until she turned and looked at it squarely and realized there was nothing behind it. Sandy no longer waited at windows. "Sometimes..." Beth began. Then she shook her head, muttering, "I don't know." From the corner of her eye, she saw the driver looking at her intently. "It's nothing. What about you? Am I taking you out of your way?"

"No. Like I said, it's on my way."

Beth braced herself against the back of the seat. The hum of the car vibrated gently through her body. There were less and less lights. Few cars passed. She couldn't see the surface of the road. Snow sprayed up from the sides of the car. It must be several inches deep, Beth thought. Maybe a foot by now. She glanced at the speedometer dreamily. They were traveling at 78 miles per hour.

Beth half twisted around in the direction of the back seat as if there was some thought left there in mid-sentence. Seeing the case, she turned back.

"Open it." The driver's eyes held Beth's forcibly. "Please."

"What?"

"The case. I want you to look inside." Beth felt the nudge of the woman's gaze. "Please," she said with a small thrust of her chin.

Was it a request or a command? Beth shrugged and twisted around in her seat, reached back and pulled the case onto her lap. The contents shifted heavily. Her hands slid over the silky leather. Her forefinger moved involuntarily to the latch. It snapped open eagerly. The lid pressed against her palm, insistent. She slid her hand away and the case opened with a sigh.

"Holy shit!" Beth's hands flew to her throat. "You rob someplace or what?"

The driver looked at Beth steadily.

"I mean . . . this is all yours? I mean the company's?" The shining, writhing clusters of gems sparked from necklaces, rings, brooches, all striking her with their various lights. She slammed it closed again.

"I know it's terribly disorganized," the driver said, glancing down at the case. Instantly, her attention shifted as she swung the steering wheel all the way to the left, then sharply back again. The car responded with the fluidity of an experienced dance partner. Beth craned her neck to see whatever caused the car to swerve. It was some animal, but she could not determine its identity. She sensed the alarm in its eyes and the attitude of its nerves and muscles, poised to flee.

"I left in such a hurry after my last appointment," the driver continued, guiding the car back into its lane. Beth twisted around in her seat to stare back at whatever had vanished in layers of white on darkness.

"What was that?" Beth asked, turning back around to face the driver.

The driver's eyes grazed the rearview mirror. She shrugged, the incident already dismissed. Beth felt a flash of anger at the driver's insouciance, the way she hardly watched the road, hardly touched the steering wheel.

Her knees shifted under the case. Irritation yanked at her. It wasn't right. The way the car accepted her; the way it swerved at incredible speeds and yet maintained the road; the soundlessly running engine. *And snow.* It hit her like the back of a hand. Her heart slammed against her chest. It was the wrong time of year for snow! "How much farther?" she asked. Panic rattled her voice and the driver turned to her with a long look of concern. A look so long, the car traveled on unguided.

"Is there someone waiting?" the driver asked again.

Apples. The ones at the top. The ones you can never quite get to. The way they look when the sun just clips them. Like something you want beyond anything else in the world.

Beth felt the touch of lights through the closed case. Her hands still rested on it. She jerked them away, then let them settle back again. She stared down at the case for a few heart beats. When she looked up into the tunnel she was traveling into, the edges of her panic had beveled, softened. She concentrated on the flakes that even at the speed they were travelling could be counted before they swept past the windshield.

For a long time she watched the snowflakes, becoming so

drowsy her mouth fell slightly open, her eyelids drooped. She heard herself speaking. "Doesn't it matter that it's the wrong season for snow?"

"What?" the driver's voice surprised her. Beth had momentarily forgotten about her.

"The wrong . . ." Beth began. She looked ahead, taken back into the intricate design of snow falling. "Sometimes," she continued, "I wake up in the middle of the night or just before morning and I'm not sure where . . . in my life . . . I am." Beth glanced over at her companion, surprised by her own words. The driver's full attention was trained on her. "Even . . . how old I am. What house I'm in. If someone is beside me. Or waiting for me. I lose my place."

The driver said nothing in reply, but Beth felt her attention just as keenly as she had felt the flight of the animal at the road side. There were no lights now, except for the headlights of the car they traveled in, boring through night. No cars passed and there was something about the space that promised nothing more would come from it. The driver was staring straight ahead, sweeping into turns at 80 miles per hour, barely guiding the steering wheel. The car floated through turns that became more and more frequent.

"Once I thought," Beth said quietly, "if I woke up and he was not there, if I should ever lose her, if I found myself alone . . ." The car swept over a hill and for an instant hung in space before it dipped to meet the road again. "But here I am," she said with a little laugh. Outside the windows, Beth could see that all boundaries of road, sky, and earth had merged.

"Open the case," the driver whispered.

It was still balanced on Beth's knees. Her hands moved over it but avoided the latch. Her heart beat faster, anticipating the touch of the lights. Very lightly, her forefinger touched the latch and the top lifted. She gasped and looked away. She could feel the cold lights reflecting blue, green, red, all over her throat.

"Choose one," the driver urged. Beth looked down at the jewelry again.

"Please," the driver prompted. "I've taken you so far out of your way."

"But . . . "

"And as you can see, there are no more stations."

"Stations?" Beth repeated wistfully. She looked out the windows and tried to find some definition to the landscape. There was nothing but whiteness now. They were no longer on the main road. She didn't remember at what point they had turned off, but it seemed they were traveling between two hills that swelled up gently from the darkness and vanished by degrees into whatever had become of the night. Distantly, Beth saw the silhouette of three twisted apple trees.

The driver stopped the car. The idling engine made an almost singing sound. "Choose," she repeated.

Beth peered into the tangle of insistent lights. "Oh, I don't know," she said fretfully, then plunged her hand into the midst of the jewelry and pulled out an opal ring. She held it up to the driver. "This one."

The driver's smile was radiant.

"Well, then," she said briskly. She shut the case and slid it off Beth's lap. Then she adjusted her skirt and hair, glanced around as if making a last inspection, and stepped out of the car. She stood knee-deep in snow. She turned, grasped the car door and stooped to wave good-bye to Beth, the snow swirling around her and into the car. "I'll be going then."

Beth gaped at her, and finally caught hold of words. "You're not . . . just. . . . Where are you going?"

"Why . . . home."

"But there's nothing here!"

The driver cocked her head indulgently, fluttered her fingers, turned and walked into the whiteness of the hill. Beth strained to watch her go, but she vanished almost immediately. Only the trees on the top of the hill stood against the whiteness. Then even the trees were gone. She could see nothing but whiteness.

Snow blew through the interior of the car, over the fine upholstery and polished wood, over her knees and the opal she held between her fingers. It was an inscrutable stone. The blue and gold lights submerged in a glabrous fog. Why, she wondered, with all there was to choose from, had she chosen this one.

Three Rowboats

I meant to write a love story but it came to this:

Three rowboats tethered to the dock, oars pulled in. They jostle one another in a tender sort of way, like horses do that are used to being stabled together. The three turn on a current imperceptible to me, always taking the same direction, as if they are of the same opinion.

When the girl untied one of the boats and rowed with the boy out to the island, didn't she know how it goes here? How the

wind comes up and turns the lake against us? The girl was frightened or very sad, the way she fumbled at the knot. Did he row
or did she? It doesn't matter now. The wind came up. It always
does. The wind came up and the two boats left at dock bucked
and reared and banged against one another.

It didn't last. It never does.

Late afternoon, the lake stilled, sunk in mountain shadow.

Out of the dark, into the light,

a boat adrift,

one oar in, one oar out, reading the current

back to its place

between.

Large

⌒

The Very Large Woman sat atop a mountain and mused upon her situation. Under the preponderance of her weight, the mountain was reduced in minutes to what several million years of erosion would do if it were to happen naturally, rather than by the Very Large Woman. But the Very Large Woman wasn't thinking about the mountain or about the devastation that followed in her wake. She was thinking that it was very lonely these days and she wondered where the others had gone.

While she thought about all this, the Very Large Woman dug her toe absently into a stream at the base of the collapsing mountain she was perched upon. It was just a trickle to the Woman, but actually it was a river, which she made into a lake, then a river again, then obliterated it completely by kicking a pile of mountain rubble over the top of it. She was puzzled by where the river, then lake, then river, had gone, and this made her wonder again about where all the people had gone, and for that matter, all the creatures that used to fly and scurry about for her enjoyment.

At first, the Very Large Woman was amused how every living thing fast enough fled from her approaching shadow. She would wander through a village, shattering dishes and domiciles along with the tiny inhabitants, and never understand why they got so mad and made all that noise down there. The birds and animals abandoned their territories in the wake of the wasteland she created wherever she passed. She would plow through forests, pulling up oaks and pines as easily and absently as you might pull up a sheath of grass during a stroll, then she'd bite off one end and scratch her head with the broken tip. She thought nothing of this, of course. What else were trees for, anyway? The Very Large Woman never meant to be the cause of all this destruction and commotion. It just seemed to happen wherever she was.

As she shuffled along through the increasingly barren landscape, she began to brood. She had not always been this lonely. She remembered with fondness, as her big toe gouged out another canyon, how she was once celebrated for her largeness. People photographed her and made movies about her. They fed her everything she liked. But then she grew too large on everything she liked. So large, that her bodily functions could wreak havoc. She would blow down walls with a sneeze. Expelled gas would poison the countryside. A quick nap would crush a town. Everywhere she went was made into memories. Everything she touched became something other than what it had been.

All this brooding made the Very Large Woman despondent as she shambled alone among memories in a place no longer filled with people or birds or animals or trees. She had been walking for a very long time hoping to find people who would feed her and take selfies with her, but there were no people to be found anywhere. She would at least like to pet a dog or touch a fish, she thought, even though they always became something else when she did that. *It isn't fair!* declared the Woman to herself, stomping her feet into the earth with such force water spouted from underground causing her to momentarily forget her loneliness as she concentrated on carving ravines and rivers out of the mud with her feet, then constructing dams and prodding avalanches.

Just as she was about to squish her toes through it all,

something flew into her eye, then into her ear, emitting an annoying high-pitched buzz. The Very Large Woman was annoyed. She had been enjoying the feel of mud between her giant toes, and swatted at the thing whizzing around her head. Finally, the noise stopped. Then she noticed a blue smudge on her palm. When she looked very closely, she saw that the smudge had been a thing called bird. *Oh, well*, she sighed, and wiped her hand on her very large thigh.

As the woman returned to her excavations, something fell from her hair onto her breast. She was about to brush it away, but because she was somewhat bored, pushed the thing onto her palm and brought it close to her face. A nest, now containing only one bird, a bald thing except for a spray of blue fuzz. It occurred to the Woman that perhaps the nest and one remaining bird were connected to the annoying thing she had recently squashed. When she thought a little further back, she realized she must have collected the nest in her hair from the last tree she had pulled up to scratch her head with—not the first time such a thing had happened. Once it was a Goshawk that kept dive-bombing her and other times it was squirrels and owls and woodpeckers which proved particularly bothersome. It was hardly worth pulling up trees anymore for all the trouble it caused her.

Anyway, back to the problem of the bird in the nest in the hand of the Very Large Woman who, you might think, would surely blow it away with one exhale, but no. The Woman stopped, held her breath. She considered how to proceed because this was the last bird she had seen in a very long time and it occurred to her that birds were getting very scarce for some reason.

She decided to save the bird. The bird would be her companion and always be grateful to her for saving it. It would perch on her shoulder and sing to her.

The bird was not easy to take, however. It peeped all the time with its little orange mouth wide open and the Very Large Woman soon tired of all the noise that did not sound one bit like singing. But the peeping was one of the few sounds of life to be found anywhere and she decided to put up with it. She knew nothing about feeding baby birds, even if it had crossed her mind to do so. But the bird was crafty and survived off the insects that smacked into the largeness of the Very Large Woman, became trapped in her hair, or bounced off her nose into the bird's constantly open beak.

Then the peeping became squawking that grew so loud the Woman could not gather her thoughts, which would have been about when the squawking would stop and the singing would begin.

Eventually the bird gained a voice that was not a peep or a squawk and was definitely not singing. "Hey, Large," he bellowed disrespectfully, "how about something a little more substantial up here." The Woman was perplexed. "Like big insects. The ones at this altitude are not filling the bill. How about bending down in that patch of green and grabbing me one of them big old fat grasshoppers."

Looking down from her considerable height, the Woman discovered that there was, indeed, a field of grasses, something not seen in a long time. However, it was *very* far down. Bending was not easy for the Woman. "I don't know," she replied uncertainly.

"Just get down on those big stumps of yours and scoop up a handful. With those huge paws, you're bound to come up with something. You don't want me to starve, do you?"

"No, no," answered the Woman, again uncertainly. But all the Woman came up with were boulders and great clumps of earth and the remnants of a turtle shell. "I'm not good at this," she moaned.

"Well," said the bird petulantly, "then I will starve and that will be the end of me. Because you do not love me enough to provide for me."

Greatly distressed, and not stopping to think why or if she loved the bird at all, the Woman tried again. And again and again. Each time she brought up great chucks of earth containing nothing living but a few worms. Finally, she captured in the midst of one of the handfuls, one maimed caterpillar which the bird hungrily devoured. This pleased her so much she pulled up acres of field until the bird stopped whining about how she didn't love him enough.

The Woman sat down on a range of hills to catch her breath, quickly reducing the hills to plateau. She was exhausted, but at least the bird was quiet. It had curled up in her hair somewhere to sleep. "I must love the bird enough now," she said to herself. "He is quiet."

But the bird was not quiet for long. He awakened early and began to sing.

"How did you learn to do that?" asked the Woman.

"It's nothing you had anything to do with," replied the bird. "When you speak trees blow down. Look at the holocaust you have created in just one day."

The Woman looked around. There was a wide trail of demolition leading up to where she sat. "But how else was I to provide for you?" she wailed.

"Perhaps if you could fly," said the bird, "you would be less of a burden on the earth. Then without a backward glance, the bird flew away from the Very Large Woman.

"Wait," called the Woman. "You can't leave me. Who will catch grasshoppers for you?"

"I can fly now. I don't need you anymore. As a matter of fact, you are a definite liability."

The woman began to see her vision of a grateful bird perched on her shoulder and singing for her delight vanish.

"I could be of use," she whimpered. But for the life of her, she could not think of how.

"Of use?" squawked the bird, fluttering around her head. "Of use! You pluck trees out of the earth, crush nests, trample fields, suck up rivers. With you plowing a path of destruction after me, I would never find a mate to raise a family. If there is any bird to find anywhere anymore!"

"But I love you," Large sobbed.

"Then," said the bird with a cock of its head, "I guess you'll have to learn to fly."

The Very Large Woman had never contemplated flight before. But the more she thought about it, the more certain she became that flight was the answer to her immense loneliness. If she could fly, she would not crush another thing and then she could follow the bird wherever the bird went and he would know she loved him because she had learned to fly. "But how?" asked The Woman, finally. She could see that nothing about her was designed for flight.

"Follow me," called the bird and he undulated into the distance, with the Woman plowing behind.

Finally, after two days of traveling, they came to a place Large had not seen before. It was very high and getting there had taken every last ounce of her strength. At the top it was windy and far below was the ocean.

"Now you must leap from the cliff and spread your arms as wide as you can and then, about halfway down, you will become airborne."

"Airborne?" questioned Large.

"Yes," said the bird. "You will be born on air, a new thing, light as a feather."

Large liked the thought of this. Borne on air. Light as a feather. Without another thought she leaped off the cliff into the sea. Of course, she was not airborne. She plummeted unceremoniously into the sea causing a tidal wave that swept over the wounded land, and eventually consumed the Woman completely with a resounding belch.

The bird hovered over the cliff for a long time to be sure that Large would not resurface.

"Love hurts," he sang in the most poignant, fluting notes, "ew, ew, ew, love hurts, so, so hurts, oh, love hurts, oh yeah."

The Nature of Things

~

I 'm grateful now for what we didn't know.

We didn't know that Maxine's 1974 Ford Pinto, a 15-year-old junker, could spontaneously explode if rear-ended. Considering my sister's driving eccentricities, that could have happened at any time. She was a lethally distracted driver—stomping on the brake should a thought sail into her head or the need to refresh her makeup, light a cigarette or twist the radio knob in search of her tunes—all of which were happening as she reached for the high note of *Blue Bayou* while negotiating New Lebanon Road, a high traffic east-west route, in search of the turnoff to Calvary Catholic Cemetery.

I grew up in Nashville, but hadn't been back since my mother's funeral two years before, a grand Irish Catholic affair, thanks to the largesse of my Uncle Liam, with all the trimmings, and held in St. Ann's Cathedral where the McMurphy clan were lifelong congregates. I don't remember anything beyond the service—the gleaming oak casket strewn with baby's breath and roses, and how the priest stumbled over his notes that held nothing about Molly McMurphy Greene, other than her standing as a good Catholic, loving mother and wife, and her acceptance into the graduating class of God's realm. The solemn occasion at the burial site is lost to me. I must have stood around the grave with my brothers, John and Mitch, Maxine and various aunts, uncles and cousins. Maxine and I got whopping drunk on the way there, so maybe that's why it's all a bit fuzzy.

Another thing about Maxine's driving: She never saw a turn coming until forced into a 90-degreer, throwing passengers against the door, thankfully secured with a bungee cord. She made just this turn into the Calgary Catholic Cemetery, non-plused by the semi, bellowing its outrage as it swerved past. She pulled over on Aisle of Ascension, dredged up a crinkled bank receipt from her purse and studied the back of it where she had apparently written the directions. "Section 15, Lot 253," she announced, looking at me as if I knew where that might be.

"By the way, you have an upside-down eyebrow." I said in a tone that was, I realized, weighted with judgement. When we were both younger, an upside-down eyebrow might have paralyzed us with laughter. She adjusted the rearview mirror, frowned at her image. "Don't you have a map of this place?" I asked, once she had located the eyebrow pencil under her butt and made rough reparations. I knew of course she did not have a map and probably not a clue and was navigating on a memory as faulty as the Pinto's transmission.

She tried once more to reach that note only Linda Ronstadt could attain. After the attempt broke down in an avalanche of discordance, she switched off the radio, and with a wrench of the parking brake, announced, "We'll find it. All the McMurphys are buried here. They own at least half an acre of this place."

Outside the car, she seemed less sure as she surveyed the up and down sweeps of the cemetery, the crosses, obelisks, the statues of saints and angels. After pacing back and forth along the road, she stood, hands on hips, summing up the landscape. I leaned against the Pinto, observing her with fraying patience as she tilted to the left, then to the right, one hand shading her eyes as if scanning the horizon for an incoming vessel. My sister, 46 years old, still dressed like a teenager—cut-off jeans, a tee-shirt declaring *I'm from New York Fucking City!* (she wasn't) and flip-flops. Her once dark blond hair was pulled back in a scorched orange ponytail. After a few moments, she swung around, wide-eyed with discovery, and pointed in the direction of a statue just downhill. "There! I know that Mary! Mol's is just over that little hill."

Leaving the Pinto on the Aisle of Ascension, we walked downhill through the early summer green, past Mary in her per-petual mourning, then over a rise beyond which, Maxine was sure, lay our mother's grave.

She paused long enough to light a cigarette, then trekked on ignoring, as she always did, my harangue on the likelihood of COPD, which had done our father in. Once we crested the knoll, she slowed, stopped, swiveled in each direction, ponytail swinging. "It was here . . ."

"Someone must have robbed it, huh? Scurried off with Mol's gravestone?"

"Don't be a shit. It's *supposed* to be here." Instead of our moth-er's grave, a formidable mausoleum rose before us, encircled by smaller stones, like chicks around a hen. "But it's not." Whatever she said after that I didn't hear. A wind came up, setting the trees to shushing, and I couldn't catch a word above them.

"Come on!" I called to her. "Let's just find the damn office or ask someone."

But there was no office, no official building in sight, and not a single living soul seemed to be visiting their dead that day. We continued past the mausoleum, crossed the drive on one of its many arcs through the cemetery and climbed a slight rise until we happened on a section marker. "Section 10," I yelled at her. "We're nowhere near the right section. A map would have helped." I glared at my sister who ignored me as she crushed her cigarette butt into the grass with the tip of her flipflop, then pulled another Marlboro from the pack tucked inside the waistband of her shorts.

"Section 15 must be that way." She nodded east, then west, the unlit cigarette bobbing from the corner of her mouth. She started off again, cutting laterally across graves, relying on nothing more than her gift for misdirection. I called for her to wait up, to locate a marker first or a fellow mourner—we couldn't be the only ones in the cemetery—but she had disappeared behind an obelisk and was only traceable by a tail of cigarette smoke. I stopped, drew in a levelling breath, looked around. It was midafternoon and the early mist had lifted. I saw through my own cloud of frustration that it was a rare day, freshly unwrapped, a day that doesn't come twice. The trees all around us—splendid, towering oaks, tulip trees, black gum and magnolia—were startlingly green, the magnolias still holding bloom. Mol would stop here, too, I thought. She wouldn't know the names of the trees, she would simply enjoy their presence, be fully aware of them. She would urge me to look up, too, be patient, and, giving me a conciliatory wink, "be kinder to your sister."

"Well, at least we're headed in the right direction now," I called after Maxine, trying to obey Mol's wishes, the least I could do. I caught sight of the top of my sister's orange ponytail in what appeared to be the farthest corner of the cemetery. Closer, I saw the ground in that section had sunken and in its lap was a small plot, surrounded by a rusted iron fence. Unlike the curated grounds surrounding it, this orphaned corner looked to have been left to return to the wild. The gate tilted off its post, the grasses, wild roses and bramble were high enough to conceal the stone my sister was kneeling before, reading the inscription with her fingertips. Atop the stone reclined the rain-pitted statue of a sleeping child, just above the reach of the overgrowth.

"Eighteen ninety-three," she read. "Sarah . . . I can't read the last name . . . *resting here in eternal peace with her stillborn sister.* That's all I can make out."

"Two kids in the same grave?"

"This is the old, old part of the cemetery. The whole family is here. Killed off by consumption or wasting disease or one of those things people got back then."

"Deer," I said. "Deer get wasting disease, not . . ."

Maxine wasn't listening. She studied each headstone, ciphering the epitaphs. I doubted she could make out more than a word or two through the patterns of moss and lichen that covered them.

Maxine had been a weird kid—histrionic, tantrum prone, and a bit ghoulish. She had a hawk's eye for abandoned cemeteries. I can still see her as an eight-year-old flattening her face against the car window, pointing out what the rest of us could not see, an overgrown family plot on a hillside or tucked within an assembly of saplings. If our father was drinking, he might indulge her, pulling over and letting her loose like a hound on scent while he dozed or smoked or retrieved a bottle of Jack Daniels from under the seat. This graveyard obsession worried Mol. She thought it could be sacrilege. It made me furious. I was the one sent after Maxine to keep her from, I guessed, being lured away by whatever spirits still lurked there. I would maintain my distance, watching in disgust and surreptitious fascination as she waded through a forest of the forgotten, reading each inscription with her fingertips as if receiving messages from the departed. I could see her lips moving as she stroked each headstone, composing fantastic stories she would chatter on about on the way home. Maxine had her own adaptation of reality.

"Let's go!" I yelled as I must have yelled back then, waiting for my sister to rise out of the shadowy clutch of gravestone and grasses. "We're here to find Mol. I'm sure she's nowhere near this section."

Maxine heard me this time. She wound her way past the graves, touching each stone, even those that were fallen and broken. She struggled to close the gate behind her, to wrench it back on its post. "I wonder . . ." she sighed, giving up on the gate, "what about babies that never become Sarahs?" She had turned back to gaze upon the plot. "The ones that don't make it. Do they get a grave? A marker? Do they get a name?" I wasn't sure who she was addressing. Maybe the Sarah on the gravestone. Maybe God. Maxine's version. She still considered herself Catholic though, as far as I knew, she hadn't attended church since our mother demanded it. She never got the rules or ceremonies right.

Even after I'd shrugged this question off as typical Maxine bathos, it hung around, pulling at some memory.

The search for our mother's grave was becoming nightmarish, like being trapped in a maze of headstones, statues, and trees with *Do they get a name?* shadowing me. I wanted to end it, scream at Maxine, but I wasn't sure if she was to blame for this staggering incompetence or if I was for trusting her. How would I explain to my family, my friends, co-workers, myself that I was too damn stupid to pay my mother this essential ritual of respect—the reason I had come to Nashville in the first place. I had an overpowering urge to catch up to Maxine, snatch her by that silly ponytail, flipping her backwards. Maybe she'd break a limb. But she had scurried ahead. When I caught sight of her, she was bent over a grave, and appeared to be praying.

"You found it?"

She had not. She was picking through irises laid across someone else's grave. I swung around, surveying the grounds for anyone else who might have witnessed this desecration, but we were in a purgatory of our own. I stood over her, pressing my telepathed outrage into the back of her head. She was choosing the choicest ones. "Mol loves irises and these are perfect— look! white, purple and yellow. She liked the purple ones best." Maxine was in a reverie of discovery until she looked up at me. "What? Did you bring flowers? No! So don't give me that look. They'll be wilted in an hour anyway." I stood over her, mouth open, incredulous. "I left most!" she added, rising with the irises cradled in her arms.

"I wonder what St. Augustine thinks of that," I nodded to the statue overlooking the grave, "or ..." I leaned down to read the name on the marble headstone, "Agnes Mahoney."

"Agnes won't mind." Maxine strode off with renewed vigor, apparently confident of Agnes' good tidings and that our mother's grave was just ahead of us. I was less sure. We were, somehow, in the right section, Section 15, but not in the right lot, and according to the back of the bank receipt that Maxine had left in the car, there were over two hundred graves in that section alone. It was getting warmer. Sweat raced down my sides.

A few cars were parked along the road, but fortunately, no one else to be seen. Maxine, prowling among the headstones, looked like a felon stooping over each one as if searching for the code to their opening. Suddenly, she straightened, gave a little hop, waved her arms at me. She had found the grave.

No, but she had found the McMurphy plot. As we inspected each headstone, I realized I did not know, and may never have heard of, most of our relatives residing there. My father had sneered at my mother's family—shanty Irish he called them, dismissing their wealth and community standing. Maxine was not the only one to have an alternate version of reality. Uncles Liam and Crocker had built the largest and most successful construction business in Nashville after returning from military service.

I was keenly jealous of my cousin Reba's tap dancing and horseback riding lessons.

There was clearly a hierarchy in the McMurphy plot. Uncle Liam and Aunt Grace had the most flaunted monuments, rising 15 feet high and just as wide, topped by a cross with the alpha omega symbols and engravings that entwined love of family, God, and country. The headstones stepped down in opulence from there, the messages less beatific. After twenty minutes of inspecting each headstone, we did not find our mother's grave. "Where's Mol?" Maxine shrieked, strangling the irises. She looked panicked, as if our mother may have been evicted from her rightful place among the sanctified.

We were looking for the wrong memorial. There was no stone, just a plaque recessed into the earth. Instead of the ecclesiastic verbiage on the other stones, the inscription was simply: Molly M. Greene, 1922 – 1994.

"Like something to wipe your feet on," Maxine puffed and sniffled like a toddler about to let loose a squall. It was clear she hadn't visited the gravesite as often as she had said, maybe not since the burial, at which she'd been as drunk as I was.

"Doesn't matter," I said, nudging her with my elbow. "Look." I pointed to a massive straight-trunked tree that threw its shadow over the grave. It soared at least 80 feet. Two horizontal branches, mid-way up the trunk and directly opposite one another, gave the tree the appearance of a cross. "That's a tulip tree, the most dominant tree in the whole God-besotted place. Mol receives its blessing every sunrise. I'd say that's better than one of these hulking monuments."

My sister, still tilting toward meltdown, looked unconvinced. She still clutched the irises, eyed the plaque doubtfully. I elbowed her again, and she threw a glance in my direction. Then, in a small, sullen voice, "So why is it called a tulip tree?"

"You have to look, Maxine!" I steered her attention back to the tree, to the top branches. It was taller than most of the trees in the cemetery, forcing us to bend backwards to see the tulip-shaped yellow blossoms near the crown.

Maxine squinted up at the tree, then dropped her eyes on me.

"You *would* know that!" She was searching my face with that quizzical half smile that augured a stirring beneath the surface. I couldn't tell what, and I was wary. "You amaze me," she said, stressing "amaze". "You went to college, got the hell out of Nashville!" She swung her free arm in a circle, taking in, I guessed, all of Nashville, the cemetery, our history. In her other arm, the drooping irises. "You, John and Mitch all left."

"You could have too . . ." and stopped there. I'd fallen into her trap.

The half-smile slid into a sneer that instantly evoked my father. "Who else would take care of them?"

I lifted a sweaty clump of hair off my forehead, took a deep breath, had no answers. How many ways had this been said—hinted, joked at, or acted out. Embedded in "who else . . . ?" a challenge no matter how it was played.

Who else but Maxine?

She could never find herself. That would be Maxine's epitaph. While my brothers and I couldn't wait to kickstart our lives elsewhere, Maxine stayed in Nashville, "freelancing" she called it, between jobs as dog walker, house sitter and bartender. She hadn't strayed farther than Memphis except once—a memorable once—the summer she turned nineteen. She simply disappeared after the late shift at the Golden Fox, where she was part-time server, bartender. No one knew where she had gone, or who she was with until she called from somewhere in Alabama. "Maxine's escapade," was how Mol referred to it.

As it turned out, it was a last blast of insurgency. Maxine returned, offering no cogent explanation, and gradually settled into the role that we all implicitly expected of her—to tend to the failing health of our parents, both of whom died within three years of one another. During our parents' last years, my brothers and I sent money and "peeked in," as Maxine used to say, to punch our cards.

It was all rising that June morning from the never quite buried. Mol would have stepped in here, assuming, as she always had, the feckless role of mediator, trying to tamp down the furies that flared among the four of us. *Stop it now,* she would say, hands fluttering, face fretted with worry. *Let's just be pleasant.*

Maxine dropped her eyes to consider her unevenly painted toenails. "Anyway . . . " she said, losing the energy to relaunch a tired grievance.

My sister was five years younger than I, and during her childhood had been a chubby, tantrum-prone menace. Somewhere along the way, she had tossed off that carapace and revealed a stunning, if a little decadent, beauty. It shocked us all. No one knew what to do with Maxine, including Maxine, who used up this bounty like a drunk on a binge. It let her down, this flash of inflorescence. She looked exhausted and, I thought, sunken.

Remembering the irises, Maxine stooped to settle them across Mol's grave. It was a gesture of such tenderness a surge of grief tightened my throat, not for my mother, but for my little sister, the way her fingertips stroked the stems of the flowers. "I guess we won't be joining the McMurphys," she said, straightening. "No more room." Then she laughed, really laughed, the old irreverent laugh.

Sunday morning mass. Those ridiculous hats Mol made us wear. She stood between us so we could not conjure conspiracies.

Our submission to the dictates and rituals of the Catholic church was the one win she managed to wrest from my father's tyranny and belittlements. Maxine and I had little appreciation for how much this cost her. We fought her, squirming against the church doctrines that laid sins like traps we were born to fall into, made us sit our skinny butts on unyielding pews, listening to undecipherable Latin, gazing at the suffering statues of Mary and Joseph and Jesus with his terrifying exposed heart. Once we caught one another's surly, bored, defiant gaze across Mol's midsection, laughter tickled our throats. We covered it with a cough, tried to dam it up until it swelled beyond our control, threatened to blow out our mouths, noses and ears. And it did, erupting in a defiance so unholy it shocked even the two of us. Mol was forced to grab us by the arms and pull us stumbling over worshipers to the end of the pew, down the aisle with all those condemning eyes upon us, and out the groaning wooden doors.

"I don't think they'd have us."

She laughed again, just a rumble, like the aftermath of thunder that had worn itself out. "How are we going to remember where Mol's grave is next time we come?"

I didn't know when I'd visit the gravesite again, but at least I knew how to find it. "The tulip tree. You can see it from the road. The tallest tree in the cemetery." Maxine looked down at the irises as if she regretted leaving them there. Then she smiled. "Let's see if we can find the car."

It took a while. Heat settled over us like a woolen blanket. I was never suited for the climate in Tennessee. Maxine claimed she loved it, but she was breathing heavily and the back of her tee-shirt was soaked through. She spoke with urgency through sporadic bursts of breath about Mol, John and Mitch, then whether the Pinto would start.

"Remember in the funeral parlor before the memorial

service," I asked when she stopped talking long enough to search for her car keys, a cover for her shortness of breath, "when they wheeled out the casket for us to have a private viewing?"

"Yeah?"

"You had a shit fit, remember? Bellowing like a lunatic: *That's not my mother!*"

"I didn't bellow. And it wasn't. They made her up like a whore!"

"I thought she looked pretty damn good."

"Oh, come on!"

"And then . . . during the memorial service . . ."

"Oh, God, yeah, we did it again."

Hemorrhaging laughter, we had staggered out as if Mol was dragging us by the elbows.

On the rise to Isle of Ascension, we stopped again. Maxine bent over, hands on her knees, trying to catch her breath. I resisted the sins of smoking lecture. Instead, I turned and sat, facing downslope, the way we had come. She settled beside me.

I was leaving the next day, dreaded Maxine driving me to the airport, which she would insist upon. This was closing time for my visit and usually I would wrap it up with a cheery platitude about next time, but I resisted that, just watched in silence as she idly picked through the grass. There are layers to people, only visible to those who love them deeply. Maxine had run through every one during my short visit.

Three notes speared the air. We looked up to see where they would land. "Cardinal," I said because I had always done that, instructed her on the nature of things. She chucked a laugh. She knew Cardinals. They had always been her favorite bird.

From the slope, we could see the shadows lengthening through the cemetery, not far enough to reach into the corner of the forgotten family plot. But it was there. The statue of Sarah.

I had not been able to leave it behind. I knew that if Maxine and I were to claim the truth between us, it was at that embryotic moment, floating between hazards. *I remember when you called from Alabama. You told me about the baby. But it was finals week. It got in my way.* But I said nothing.

"I used to reach that note," she said, tilting her face up at me. "Remember? You never could." Before I could remind her neither of us ever could, she got to her feet, brushed off the back of her shorts.

We found the Pinto, parked like an obedient horse. For a moment, we lingered on Aisle of Ascension, thinking about when the next time would be. We didn't know that Maxine had already developed nodules on her lungs.

Before we got in the car, I turned and pointed out the crown of the tulip tree, our navigational point for next time, or at least I think it was the same tree. I told her it was, anyway.

The Deconstruction of Eza, 1959

~꙳~

I t's always an event when Aunt Eza comes to Sunday dinner. While Mom watches over her kettle of ham hocks and green beans, my brother Lewis and I wait at the front window for Eza's arrival. Uncle Dean will be dropping her off, since Eza doesn't drive, and retrieve her two hours later, after the Sunday ballgame he watches with his brother, Earl, who he doesn't particularly get along with but Earl owns the only TV set in the family.

Lewis and I watch as Eza unfolds her volumes of skirts, scarves and furs from the white Cadillac and, once she has all of herself composed outside of it, walks carefully up the slope to the house, stops, wobbles back to the car and closes the door, gathers herself, adjusts her columns of hair, starts toward the house again. This all takes about ten minutes, long enough for us to gauge if she is nipping. She is always a little unsteady on her feet given the weight of her assemblage.

As soon as Eza arrives, it becomes evident how small the kitchen is. "Ohhhh, you're getting so pretty," she chirps, clutching me to her bosom. I'm not, and know it very well. She turns to the left and right, then does a stumbling twirl around the room. "And where is that Leweegie?" Lewis shuffles out of the living room, shy, awkward, grinning, then grimaces in her smothering embrace. When she turns her attention to Mom, she is brought to tears, "And my little Maggie . . ." she wails as she envelopes her sister.

Eza comes every Sunday to dinner, and each time she sees us it is the first time all over again. Like all the Ryan sisters, Eza is easily overtaken by emotion. She wipes her eyes and dislodges a false eyelash, then stares down at her palm in wonderment and announces, "I'll just step into the 'bootwa' and fix myself." As she swishes and bumps her way into the bathroom, Mom's eyes follow her with a hint of concern.

By the time Eza emerges from the bathroom it is obvious she has been nipping. Thus, follows the deconstruction of Eza. After several trips to the "bootwa" she will slowly come undone. Lipstick and eyeliner will have been reapplied, but miss their targets, a bosom will appear to have slid to her waist, one of her eyelashes will be lost and she will drop one of her hairpieces into the plate of ham hocks and green beans, then absently place it in her pocketbook. Through all this, will be tears and apologies, and Mom will attempt to put her sister back together again as she has since childhood, with tenderness and compassion that will take my brother and me many years to understand.

Necessity

A dream of cold. Snow fallen all night. The horses left out, no hay thrown to them, the trough frozen to the bottom. Backlit by morning sky, they gather at the gate into their own geology. Peaks of ears, clouds of breath. Waiting.

He awakens into smothering heat and the swamp of difficult breathing. Even within the darkened room, the surge of another day pulls him to alertness. For hours he is witness to the progression of light, the surfacing of walls, the hallways coughing and groaning awake. What is the color of the walls? he asks himself each morning, angry all over again at its elusiveness. A bloodless beige like nothing in nature. The color of hospital waiting rooms and doctors' offices. Non-committal. If it tells him anything it is that he has come this far and will go no farther. All of what he carried will pass on to someone else. He tries to remember who. He leafs past Ellen, long dead, past his daughter in another state, and comes to his son. His son is taking care of everything. Everything. What is that now? Not the pigs, the chickens, the herd, the wood to get in, the hay to cut, the dog. There is just the barn now. And the horses.

One dark form rolling into the next, solidifying into a hunger mountain. There is no whinny of welcome nor blow of impatience. They draw him by the keenness of their attention. They are aware of his first stirring, the coming to wake. The stumbling down stairs into the groove of everyday. Smoke rising from the chimney, the door opening. His burdened answer to this necessity, following the same path from house to barn he has always taken, the path that is worn into him so deeply nothing else will grow there.

The carts rattle, the aides complain. At half past eight his breakfast clatters in through the doorway. An aide switches on the voice and smile she uses when entering the room. More often now, it is not thrown on until halfway across the room and is dropped before she turns around to rattle out. The aides use the same smile and voice when tending to the man on the other side of the room, his bed separated by a pale blue curtain. Not really a man, but the husk of a man, who comes back to life each morning with a howl. The sound is all the man has left of himself. He is heavily drugged and most of the time can only manage a whimper or a few weary rumbles of outrage. Three times a week, after they feed the man his breakfast, he is dressed, hoisted from his bed with a special lift and set in a wheelchair. Then he is wheeled downstairs. Two hours later they wheel him back.

He knows only this about the man: the path he will take each day. It is part of his own path now. It begins with the rise and advance of light across the room, the day put up and broken down, the new seasons of therapies and medications and the times they wheel him down to the first floor community room and park him in front of the platform where an Elvis impersonator flounces for an hour. He knows how the building sighs as it shifts from one department of the day to another. It is what he does. What he has always done. Listen for the next thing coming.

He could hear a calf being born, the hunker of a coyote, the terror held in the hen's throat, the conspiracies of weather. He heard the ice rasping on the roof that morning before it made a sound. He heard it coming while Ellen slept deeply beside him, and he heard what would come after. Power out for nine days and a herd to milk by hand. Breaking ice off the pond. He and Ellen and the kids huddled around the woodstove, making do. They always could. How did they? All those mornings, 75 head, the fields to mow, the tractor seized up, two kids to raise. Fences always down, the barn to keep up. No matter what, the barn to keep up. It held the center. The fields and pastures radiated from or rose to meet it. A 17th-century threshing barn, turned dairy barn, still as square as a good bull, its understory moored deep into earth on a fieldstone foundation.

Slates come off every spring, he tells his son. Ice works up under them all winter so a strong wind can kick them lose. Keep an eye out, he said, and tell the girl who feeds the horses to close the barn doors tight or the wind will tear them off. His son nods. She's still coming, every day, that girl who said she would? His son nods, but doesn't look at him. He is older somehow, the top of his head a pink bowl. He asks his son again, feeling that old necessity working its way into his blood, drumming his heart faster than it should go. Check the fences by the road. Every winter the snowplow knocks out rails. Horses go mad in spring; they'll find a down rail. His heart beats faster. Will the hay hold 'til grass? His son draws a long breath of exhaustion, finally looks up. Eyes sagging with too much to carry. Is the girl coming?

His son leaves, comes back another time. The aides rattle in and out. He listens to the day roll by on the commotion of wheels, shuffle of feet, the desultory savagery of the aides' conversation outside in the hallways. Smiles put on and pulled off, words wobble like jello. No one tells him anything. No one sees him. He is a child, going backwards to death. He follows the path of each day. Listens. When he comes to the hush that sinks between the joints of the day, he listens harder.

He saw no good to them. Two geldings and a lame mare. When he tries to remember how old they are, he gets lost somewhere else. No one farmed with horses, he argued. They had no more use than a barn full of kangaroos. Something else to feed. But Ellen would have her horses. She was hard on this. He never understood what it was. Any chance, she'd be off on the bay gelding without a word to anyone, away from work, out of the reach of their calls. He'd catch sight of her breaking away from the circle of need, into the north field at a canter, galloping up into the hemlock hill. One winter day—how long ago?—snow belly deep to the horse, twin black flames of her loose hair and the gelding's tail flickering away. The only dark, moving thing, like a vessel sailing toward an impossible destination, caught in a wind-whipped swirl of snow, disappeared completely.

As a boy he learned horses, but left off them when he drove his first tractor. Ellen came to horses late and grew into them. More with every year until it seemed they were all she saw. At stray moments of the day, he'd find her leaning against the fence, looking out into the field where the horses grazed. Toward the end, that was all she could do. Watching them with a look too far for him to get to.

Take care of the horses. You'll do that, won't you?

He said he would, but never meant to. With Ellen gone, the herd sold off, he'd sell the farm. But it never came to that. He could not see himself any other place. He was framed by the hedgerow of black locusts to the south, with the layering of fields beyond, the rise of the Adamowski fields to the east, the dark tide of hemlock to the north and to the west, where the weather came. The barn in the center.

Sometimes he wonders about the howling man on the other side of the blue curtain. What hills had framed him; what was his center? He wants to tell the man that he holds the same howl inside, but cannot let it out. There is no reaching the man to say anything to him. His eyes are sunken deep into his head and his cheek bones are like cliffs falling off into the cave of his mouth. No one comes to visit him.

Toward the last, there were only the horses to keep him to his old path. Just as the sun eased over the Adamowski hill and crossed the road into his own fields, he answered the call only he could hear. The path is worn there still, he knows, the 500 feet from house to barn, as deep as the paths the horses wore out to pasture. Even here, from behind these walls, he feels the way, goes there to the horses waiting. Their alertness still tuned to him. The old ache in the crook of his back as he slides the great doors open. The horses brought in, stomping over the stone floor, snorting, tossing their heads, pushing past one another. Snow on their backs, muzzles frosted.

His son in the doorway the next time. Snow steaming off his coat and hat. He can smell the depth of cold. Winter again? He almost asks, but catches himself. His mind staggers back trying to find the day before. It was summer, last time. How could he get so lost? He kept such careful track of the departments of each day, the measure of each season. He says little while his son tells him about what couldn't be helped, traffic and shifts at the mill. So long since his last visit. And yet, hadn't his son sat right there with the same explanations, the same way of mumbling into his hands, last week? He looks through the section of window visible from his side of the room. Snow falling through bare limbs. It is slanting in from the east, a needle fine snow, driven to lay the world to rest. The old necessity yanks at him. Watch the snow on the barn roof, he says. When you open the doors, it will avalanche off those slates. Bury you alive. Tell the girl to bring the horses in for the night. Don't wait too long. This one has intentions. He is studying the snow so intently he doesn't notice that his son has stopped talking and is staring at him with the obliqueness of a stranger. Then his son drops his head, speaks into his hands again. Everything is fine. It does not stop snowing. Even after darkness, the day all shut down, the snow falls.

Hissing all night across the tin roof. Were the horses in? Quickly, he is out of bed and dressed. Downstairs. Doesn't stop to rouse the fire. He switches on the porch light and there is only snow. The outline of the barn barely visible through the smothering white of sky and earth. Snow to his knees, seeping into his boots. He can hardly move against it; each step tears at his chest. The barn surfaces. Beyond is blankness. Nothing else. He stands before the barn, breathing heavily. Waiting. His breath and the scything of snow is all there is. But he knows they are there, even before he sees them. One, then the other, steps forward, assembles into the landscape he knows. He moves against the gathering snow. Slides open the door.

The Night Before Haying

~

M elinda and I stood straight as soldiers at the far end of
the field watching the kitchen light blinking. We should
have been under that light, but the moon had whispered and the
grasses were high.

A perfect harvest, he said. *The timothy ripe for cutting.*

Each stem fired, seed heads burst, tickling our palms and
swishing against our chests just coming into bloom. Melinda
had moon all over her and I laughed and touched her face to
believe it. All we ever wanted was to run. The moon, the grass,
the night. I grabbed her hand and we ran, broke apart, ran as
hard as we could through the middle of the field, our bare legs
setting the grasses to sing, to gospel, to send bobolinks to flee,
save their young.

Harvest was the end of things.

We cut black, savage craters through the heart of it. No
more a perfect harvest, but a scream against the light that spread
to the porch, outlining the man who stood there, as we struggled
for breath, laughing anyway.